There I Find Happiness

Strawberry Sands Book Ten

Jessie Gussman

Published By: Jessie Gussman

Contents

Acknowledgements

Cover art by Kim Killion of The Killion Group
Editing by Heather Hayden
Narration by Jay Dyess
Author Services by CE Author Assistant

Listen to the unabridged audio for FREE performed by Jay Dyess on the Say with Jay channel on YouTube. Get early access to all of Jay's recordings and listen to Jessie's books before they're available to the general public, plus get daily Bible readings by Jay and bonus scenes by becoming a Say with Jay channel member .

Chapter 1

"Do you think he's looking at me?"

Sally looked over to where her friend, Norma Jean, indicated.

Peter Slessing stood on the sidewalk outside of the diner in Strawberry Sands, lifting his face to the wind and gazing out on the beautiful blue waters of Lake Michigan.

"I can't tell," Sally said sincerely from where she stood, two steps up on the ladder, hooking a string of lights to a post.

She and Norma Jean were helping to decorate for the Beach Bash that Strawberry Sands was putting on to celebrate the end of summer.

Not that Strawberry Sands really was happy about the end of summer. Since it meant the end of tourist season and the end of good business and lots of tourist dollars.

Although the town would be much quieter from here on out, and Sally wasn't upset about that.

At her job as an accountant at the inn on the edge of town, things would definitely be slowing down. She already didn't have as many hours as what she needed since her Aunt Wilma had passed away and she lost her caregiving job. Not that she'd only cared for her Aunt Wilma for the money. She'd loved the lady. Although Sally had gotten a little crazy there for a bit when she'd been stuck inside doing nothing but taking care of her twenty-four hours a day, seven days a week.

She'd done one of the silliest things she'd ever done in her life during that time, and it involved her best friend, Norma Jean.

"I think he is. I think he might be coming this way!" Norma Jean's voice contained thrilled excitement.

Ever since Sally had tried to set Norma Jean and Peter up, Norma Jean had been infatuated with the man.

Peter seemed, if not oblivious, only casually interested, and not the kind of interest that made a man propose marriage.

But Sally could never tell Norma Jean that, because Norma Jean was more than just casually interested. She was obsessed with Peter.

"How's my hair look? I wore this shirt because I thought it made my eyes look more blue, but...does it make me look sallow?" Norma Jean's voice held an edge of panic, and Sally tried to infuse calmness into hers.

"You look amazing. As you always do."

Norma Jean had been blessed with beautiful looks, golden hair that flowed in perfect waves past the middle of her back, along with sultry blue eyes and a perfect bone structure.

She was curvy in all the right places, and she turned more than a few heads.

Unfortunately, her personality didn't always match her looks.

"Quick! Get down!"

"From the ladder?" Sally said, confused.

"Yes!" Norma Jean tugged on Sally's shirt, pulling her down and almost making her lose her balance.

"I'm coming," Sally said, somehow allowing Norma Jean's panic to infuse into her own voice. "What's the matter?"

"I need it! If I get up, I can accidentally fall as soon as Peter walks by. Hurry up. I can't fall if you don't move! And if we don't hurry, he'll know we switched on purpose."

He was probably already going to know. The man was less than fifty feet from them, and he would need to walk by if he continued to follow the sidewalk to the sand.

The party was at the edge of town, and the people of Strawberry Sands had been working for days. All of it had been headed up by Eleanor, Sally's friend who had done such a great job on the first annual barn dance last Christmas.

That had been such a raging success that the town had decided to do something like that for the tourists who came every summer.

They hadn't gotten organized in time to do it during the summer, so they decided to celebrate the end of summer.

They were expecting a huge turnout and were hoping to make a good bit of money off of it, enough to hopefully tide everyone over until the next tourist season.

Money might have been the first consideration, but the town wanted everyone to have a good time as well.

And they were pulling out all the stops. They had some big donations, and the decorations were fantastic. The food would be top-notch too, since Griff, who cooked at the diner and owned it with his wife, would be making most of it.

In fact, once Sally was done hanging these lights, she and Norma Jean had planned to stop in at the diner to taste his strawberry cream cheese cobbler. He'd already made three different versions of it, each one better than the last, and Sally could only imagine what this latest version tasted like. If there was any left when she got there.

And if Norma Jean didn't break something when she was trying to fall off the ladder.

"Do you think this is a good idea?" Sally said as Norma Jean scurried up the ladder, the high-heeled sandals she wore making her wobble dangerously.

"Of course! He's barely looked at me since the barn dance. I've got to do something to catch his attention." She looked over the crowd, her eyes searching until they landed on Peter.

Sally opened her mouth, but Norma Jean hissed, "Be quiet! I don't want him to know that we planned this. Not until later. Then I'll tell him, and he'll be amazed at the great lengths I'll go to grab his attention. It will impress him, and we'll tell that story to our great-great-grandchildren."

Sally closed her mouth and held on to the ladder, praying Norma Jean didn't hurt herself.

Also, she was thankful that people's thoughts didn't actually get written in a bubble above their head. If they did, Peter would probably be running in the opposite direction the second he realized that Norma Jean not only had them married but had them pegged as great-great-grandparents.

Sally didn't know a whole lot about men, but she was pretty sure that would be enough to scare almost anyone off. Actually, if some man looked at her and thought about their grandchildren, it would scare her.

Regardless, Norma Jean seemed oblivious to that type of thing. Maybe it was because she was so focused on herself, Sally wasn't sure, but they'd been friends since kindergarten, and Sally loved her, even if she wasn't the easiest person in the world to get along with most of the time.

"All right. Get ready to catch me. I don't actually want to get hurt," Norma Jean hissed, and her voice must have been loud enough to carry to the unsuspecting Peter, since he turned his head and tilted it a little, a friendly smile on his face, only his eyes weren't focused on Norma Jean. He was looking at Sally.

Peter was rather handsome, and she'd had a couple conversations with him. She definitely liked him and would have been interested in him herself, if it hadn't been for Norma Jean.

Well, that and the fact that Peter owned a farm outside of Strawberry Sands, and Sally wasn't exactly farm girl material.

She was an accountant, and she loved her job. She'd quit her job in Chicago in order to care for her Aunt Wilma, but sitting inside, manipulating numbers, drooling over spreadsheets, and creating her own formulas was her idea of a good time.

Not looking at the back end of a cow and dodging the stuff that came out of it.

Of course, Norma Jean didn't exactly seem like that kind of girl either, but that was none of Sally's business. If Peter wanted to choose someone like Norma Jean as a wife, she supposed it would be his responsibility to train her in whatever duties she would be expected to perform on the farm.

Norma Jean probably hadn't thought that far ahead, and Sally hadn't wanted to say anything to destroy the castles that Norma Jean had built in the air, all around Peter. Reality would come crashing in soon enough.

"Peter! Oh, yoohoo, Peter!" Norma Jean's shrill voice seemed to carry over the crowd and be amplified.

Peter's friendly smile wobbled a bit as his eyes shifted from Sally up to Norma Jean. He grimaced as his eyes widened, and later, Sally apologized profusely to Norma Jean because she was so busy looking at the stubble on Peter's jaw and the angled line of his nose that she forgot that she was supposed to have her arms out ready to catch her best friend as she fell off.

She only remembered as Norma Jean tumbled down on top of her, and they both fell to the ground. At least Sally did her job a little, by cushioning Norma Jean's fall.

Unfortunately, she sprained her own ankle in the process, as sharp pain shot up her leg, and her eyes flashed red and black.

"Oh," she groaned.

"You were supposed to catch me!" Norma Jean hissed at her before she turned to Peter with one arm held out. "Oh, Peter, could you please help me. I'm afraid I might have hurt myself," she said, in a completely different tone than the one that she had just used on Sally.

In the meantime, Sally bit back another groan. She didn't want to take Peter's attention off Norma Jean and put it on her. Norma Jean would be furious with her, if Peter ended up helping Sally because Sally hadn't been paying attention and allowed Norma Jean to fall and actually got hurt herself.

She could only imagine Norma Jean's reaction to that.

So she swallowed the groan and winced as Norma Jean's elbow dug into her ribs as she angled herself to reach out to Peter.

"Sally. It looks like your foot bent awkwardly underneath you. Are you okay?"

"I'm fine," Sally said, trying to keep her voice steady and not allow the pain she felt to come out in her tone.

"Peter. What about me? Didn't you see my foot twist awkwardly?" Norma Jean said, waving the hand that Peter still had not grasped.

"No. I missed it." Peter grabbed a hold of her hand and yanked up. In Sally's estimation, he didn't do it very gently but not as hard as what Norma Jean seemed to indicate, as she stumbled forward and crashed into his chest, her arms somehow going around him as she smashed the rest of herself up against him.

"Oh my goodness. I think I did twist my ankle just slightly. I don't seem to be able to put any weight on it. At all," Norma Jean said as one hand trailed down Peter's cheek and the other continued to hold tightly to him, while she kept her right foot held up in the air as though it hurt.

"That's funny. You landed on your left side. I would have thought that would have been the foot that hurt," Peter said as he held his hands up in the air, as though he wasn't sure what to do with them. His chin picked up several notches, but he seemed to be gazing down over his nose at Sally and not Norma Jean. At least, that's what it looked like when she glanced up. She only did it for a second, because she had to focus on rolling over, putting both hands on the ground, and pulling her good leg under-neath her.

She grabbed the rung of the ladder and started to push up.

"Are you okay? Can I give you a hand?" Peter said as she continued to try to pull herself to her feet, and Norma Jean continued to press herself against him.

Normally Peter was known as jovial and goofy, but he seemed rather serious today. Or maybe it was because he wasn't used to having two women falling at his feet in front of him, and it scared him.

Sally snorted, even though the pain from her ankle pressed up her leg and out both elbows.

"Thank you. I... I just thought it'd be fun to lean on the ladder and make sure that it was still sturdy. I don't want someone to get hurt and it to be our fault."

She couldn't think of any other excuse off the top of her head for why she would be slowly using her hands to climb up the ladder while not using one foot.

"You're not putting any weight on that foot. Why not?"

"I often enjoy hopping around on one leg. I find it...helps me balance when I'm on ladders in the air," Sally said, feeling stupid, because she wasn't good at making up stories on the spot. She'd never been a great liar, and this felt danger-ously close to being not only a lie but a completely unbelievable lie, which were the worst kind of lie. Although, Norma Jean had often coached her to tell the most outrageous lie she could possibly think of and then just pretend it was true.

"Oh, Peter. Oh my goodness. I think I... I feel faint. Could you help me over to that bench, please?"

The newly installed benches lined the sidewalk up and down the street of Strawberry Sands. They were a great addition, as were the shade trees that had been planted near each bench.

They were just saplings, but someone with a lot of foresight had taken the first steps that would make downtown

Strawberry Sands a beautiful place to be, in ten or fifteen years.

Not that it wasn't now, but it certainly would be even more wonderful once the trees had grown up.

"I'm pretty sure you were limping on your right leg before. But now it's your left."

"That's because you said I landed on my left side, so it must have been my left foot that got hurt!" Norma Jean said, stomping her foot on the ground. Her left foot.

"You walked on both of them with no problem. I think you're fine."

"I'm not fine. That's exactly what I've been trying to tell you!" Norma Jean draped herself over Peter, with one arm behind him, one arm gripping his front, while she again hopped on her left foot, holding her right foot in the air.

"Let me help you over," Peter finally said, walking toward the bench and bending down so she dropped on it with a plop.

Her hands must have become untangled, and Peter jumped back.

"Let me see to your friend, and I'll be back."

By this time, Sally had gotten up and stood, still gripping the ladder.

She tried putting a little weight on her right foot, but the pain had gotten so bad she was afraid she was going to

black out. So she lifted it up immediately.

But now, with Peter walking toward her, she kept both legs so the bottoms of her feet touched the ground, even though she wasn't putting any weight on her right foot.

Hopefully she could fake it until she made it. That should keep Norma Jean from being upset with her.

"I'm fine. You can take care of Norma Jean. I... I was just going to stand here and enjoy the view for a little bit."

"Once you walk on that foot."

"I will. I'll walk on it a lot. In fact, I think I might run up to the diner. I was excited about the strawberry cream cheese cobbler, and that's enough to make anyone run. Even though I'm not normally a runner." Sally clamped her mouth shut. She had a tendency to ramble on when she shouldn't.

But she also had a tendency to be nice to the point of being what Norma Jean called a doormat. She didn't really see a problem with being nice. She saw more of a problem with taking advantage of people who were nice. But that wasn't her area. Her area was just to be kind, since that's what God's command was. And she wasn't commanded to police anyone who wasn't following what the Bible said.

"I'm not normally a runner either, but I feel the same way about strawberry cream cheese cobbler. Would you be interested—"

"Oh my goodness. Look at the time. Norma Jean!" Sally said, interrupting Peter who seemed to be on the verge of asking her to head to the diner and eat with him. Norma Jean would go ballistic if she heard that. Especially when she was over there waiting for Peter to get back to her. She'd never talk to Sally again.

"Norma Jean! Didn't you say that you had to be down at the band practice at twelve o'clock?"

"No. It was one thirty," Norma Jean said, scrunching up her face like she was thinking about it.

"No. I'm sure you said it was twelve o'clock," Sally said, trying to look around

Peter to give that look to Norma Jean. The look that said if she wanted to go with Peter, she needed to pretend to need to get to band practice. Sally wasn't very good at that look. She wasn't very good at subtlety at all. She was much more of a straightforward, I'll just be nice to everyone, I don't want to make any waves, I'd rather be kind, kind of person.

"Oh!" Norma Jean said, jumping up, running over, and grabbing onto Peter's arm. "I totally forgot about that. Oh, Peter, I need you to help me walk to the grandstand where the band is practicing. Please. I don't want to be late."

"I don't see anyone over at the grandstand." Peter gave Sally a look, and Sally thought that maybe he seemed a little disappointed.

Disappointed because she was friends with Norma Jean? Or disappointed because he had hoped to go to the diner with her?

She wasn't sure. And she had to dismiss it. There was no way she could have anything to do with Peter while she and Norma Jean were friends and Norma Jean was infatuated with him.

She wouldn't do that to her friend. Peter was off-limits to her.

"Please. Can you please help me walk over? I just don't think I can do it on my own," Norma Jean said as she slipped her arm around Peter's waist and started to limp toward the grandstand. Peter had no choice but to follow along with her, steadying her.

"I'd appreciate it if you take care of that foot. Get it looked at," Peter said over his shoulder.

Sally nodded, not looking at his face, but rather her eyes were caught on the hand that hung at his waist. It was big and brown, with long fingers, a hand that knew how to work.

She liked that kind of hand.

But she stared at it for a few moments before she remembered what she'd just thought. Peter was off-limits to her.

Chapter 2

Peter walked reluctantly away from Sally. He was pretty sure that Sally's foot was hurt a lot worse than anything that might have happened to Norma Jean. After all, Sally had landed on the bottom, and from where he stood, it looked like her foot twisted underneath her. He hadn't seen her putting any weight on it.

Norma Jean was just faking it, but he wasn't sure exactly why. It was annoying the way she was clinging to him and pretending so much. Like he didn't have a brain. But maybe he didn't, since he had enough brain to figure out that she wasn't really hurt but not enough brain to figure out why she was pretending.

Regardless, he couldn't make Sally admit that her foot hurt, and he couldn't make her do anything about it when she refused to admit that there was a problem to begin with.

Sally was a mystery to him, his opposite in a lot of ways, although she rendered him speechless when he was around her.

Not speechless. He just wasn't able to summon up his normal sense of humor. He supposed she made him nervous because he wanted to make a good impression on her. But she seemed uninterested. Or maybe he knew that she was rather serious herself, and he tried to tone down the part of his personality that might not mesh with hers.

Regardless, he thought that they'd get along well together if she'd ever pay any attention to him, but most of the time, she refused to look at him, although she was friendly with everyone else.

"Oh. Maybe it wasn't twelve o'clock," Norma Jean said as they reached the bandstand which was completely deserted. She turned and blinked her big blue eyes at him. "How about we go and get some of that strawberry cream cheese cobbler? That sounded really good. I'll even let you sit beside me." She winked at him. And he wasn't sure what he was supposed to do or say to that.

It felt a little...weird.

"I think I don't really want to do that. But you go on ahead."

"Oh, but I need you to help me. Plus, you just told Sally you loved it."

"I forgot that I wasn't hungry."

"Oh, you always have room for dessert." She wiggled her brows at him.

He wondered if there was supposed to be a second meaning to the word "dessert" and he was missing it. Surely she didn't mean—

"I'll let you nibble on my neck," she said with a giggle that he thought might have been faked, but he wasn't entirely sure.

He tried to suppress his shudder.

"No, thank you." His mom had taught him to be polite, and he thought that the only thing he could have added would have been a "ma'am," which in Michigan, "ma'am" was often considered an insult. It made young women feel old, and he'd almost been slapped twice before he quit saying it.

Still, what he said still offended Norma Jean, and she wrinkled her nose, putting her hands on her hips and planting her feet.

"Fine. I didn't want to spend any more time with you, Peter Slessing, anyway.

You're going to have to do a lot of groveling if you want me to forgive you for this," she said, and she stomped her foot for good measure.

His brows furrowed as he looked at her. She was kinda cute, with her big blue eyes and her long golden hair. Beautiful actually. Sweet and curvy in all the right places, he supposed, but she just didn't do anything for him. He didn't really like the way she tried to manipulate him into doing whatever it was that she wanted him to do, and he really didn't like the way that she didn't even care that Sally might have been hurt. She wanted all the attention to herself and actually tried to keep him from helping Sally.

Of course, Sally's mouse brown hair and her nondescript eyes that weren't gray, but weren't really brown either, were far more interesting to him. Even if she wasn't classically beautiful the way Norma Jean was. He loved her willingness to help and her loyalty. Anyone who could be friends with someone like Norma Jean as long as Sally had been friends with her—and at least from the rumors around town, he'd heard that they'd been friends since elementary school—had to be loyal. She also had to be willing to put up with a lot.

Norma Jean was enough to grate on his last nerve.

But Sally seemed to love her. Seemed to be protective of her and seemed to help her however she could.

Good for Sally, but not so good for him, since he ended up stuck with Norma Jean when he'd rather be with Sally. Now Norma Jean was looking at him, giving him the hairy eyeball, and he had no idea what he'd done. He'd been polite.

"I'm sorry that you're going to be mad at me for a while. Let me know when you're done." He nodded his head and turned and walked back toward the ladder that she had fallen from.

Sally was nowhere in sight, and while he was disappointed, he hoped she'd hobbled off and gotten some help for that ankle. At the very least, she needed to sit down, take her weight off it, prop it up, and put some ice on it.

As he walked by the diner, he peered in, checking to see if Sally was sitting in there, but she wasn't, so he walked on up the street, then took a left and walked toward his brother's hotel.

He needed to talk to Franklin. That was the whole reason that he'd come into town. He hadn't realized there was going to be a big shindig that evening. He'd been so busy on the farm he hadn't made it into town for more than two weeks, and being that it was summer and everything was busy, he wasn't in a big rush. Now that the tourist season was officially over, he'd be around more. As much as the farm would let him. Which, honestly, wasn't much.

Seems like the more he did, the more there was to do. But he was slowly turning the farm profitable. At least he thought so. If he could make sense of his books.

His brother's hotel appeared as he walked past the buildings that lined Main Street, and he admired the landscaping around it, happy for his brother that he seemed to be able to make a business out of nothing. He also had been able to snag a really great wife, somehow.

Peter still didn't know what Eleanor saw in Franklin, but they seemed happy together. Maybe something had happened when they were snowed in that made Eleanor feel like she had to marry him out of pity.

Peter laughed to himself a little. He'd been ribbing his brother about that for a long time, and his brother just smiled. Which made Peter believe that there was some truth to the idea.

Really, though, he was happy for his brother.

He didn't need to go the whole way to the hotel, since as he was walking up, he saw his brother and his wife sitting on a bench outside with their lunch in their laps.

It was a beautiful day to eat lunch together, and for some odd reason, Peter felt a frisson of jealousy go through him.

He was happy for his brother, truly he was, but he supposed it would be really nice to be able to spend a day like today with someone he loved.

Not someone like Norma Jean.

He tried to make himself think nice thoughts about her. Somewhere, someone could truly love her for who she was. Unfortunately, or maybe fortunately, that man wasn't him. Still, he shouldn't wish ill on her, and he said a small prayer that she would find a wonderful lifetime love for herself. As long as it wasn't him, he had to tack on at the end. Sometimes God worked in mysterious ways, but in this case, God wasn't going to work in any way. Not between him and Norma Jean.

Apparently not between him and Sally either, although Peter wouldn't mind if that happened.

"Hey there, beautiful day," he said as he came upon his brother and his wife.

They both looked up and smiled at him.

"You can join us," Eleanor invited.

Franklin gave her an annoyed look, and Peter understood Franklin didn't want his time with his wife interrupted. Even for his brother.

"Thank you, I think I will," Peter said, smiling a little at the annoyed look his brother gave him as he sat down. He wasn't planning on staying long, just long enough to ask for his brother's advice.

"Would you like some lunch?" Eleanor asked, seeming pleased that he joined them. She truly was a wonderful woman, and he wasn't quite sure what she saw in his brother.

"No. Thanks. I'm not hungry, and I really am not going to bother you long," he assured her. But she didn't look relieved, which made him think that maybe she didn't mind his company that much.

Sally was her friend, and it was kind of tempting to ask her to put in a good word for him. Or at the very least, to try to make a good impression so she'd say something nice about him.

But that wasn't his mission for today.

"How are things going on the farm?" Franklin asked casually, talking about business the way the brothers often did.

Their parents had been big business people, and they had inherited a sizable nest egg.

Peter just couldn't get interested in the business side of things. He'd much rather work with his hands, and his inheritance had enabled him to get a good start on farming. But that didn't mean that he didn't want to make sure that his business was profitable. That much had been drummed into his head since he was in diapers.

"I need some help with my finances. I think I'm profitable, but—"

"But you never could tell the front side of a spreadsheet from the backside."

"There's a backside?"

His brother laughed. "Like I said. Clueless."

"And I know it. So, now that I'm established, and I have things working pretty well, I need to hire someone to help me figure things out. Do you know any good accountants?"

"In other words, do I know any accountants who still have hair that they're able to pull out because they'll need it if they're going to be looking at your spreadsheets?"

"Yeah. Pretty much. I'd like to have an accountant with hair, although I don't discriminate against bald people as a general rule."

"Good to know," Franklin said, rubbing a hand over the top of his head which had much less hair on it than it used to.

Peter smirked. They'd both taken after their father, who had been bald by the time he was fifty.

Peter didn't particularly care, except he figured that would make him less marketable and if he wanted a wife, he probably ought to get one while he still had hair to help him, since he needed all the help he could get.

"So, can you point me in the right direction at least?"

"I actually know someone right now who's looking for more hours. With the slowdown of the tourist season being over, I think they'll be able to give you at least twenty hours a week. Do you think that'll be enough?"

"It'll probably hurry me to keep someone busy for twenty hours, once they get everything figured out. Although, getting things figured out could take until next summer, which might give someone a good job in the off-season."

"All right then. I'll talk to them tomorrow and let you know. Actually, if they're interested, I might just go ahead and send them out."

"That's fine. They can look me up on the farm. Or give them my number. Or send them to the office. It's up to you. I'm usually at the office in the morning after the work's done, and I try to make myself stay there until lunch, although I'm not always successful."

"All right. Between nine and noon is a good time for them to show up then."

"That's right. I can put them right to work. They won't have to worry about being bored."

"Okay then. You are coming tonight, right?" Eleanor said, injecting into their conversation now that they had the accountant thing settled.

"No. Last time I went to one of those shindigs, I almost ended up getting hitched. In fact, Franklin did."

"And that's a bad thing?" Eleanor said with her brows way up and lowering her head, like a charging bull, although not exactly. But Peter knew the look.

"No. That's a great thing. Excellent. Really. Probably the best thing that ever happened to him." He said it in a fake sarcastic voice, and Eleanor laughed.

"Good answers. Good, good answers."

"I have great survival instincts."

"He had to, growing up with me," Franklin said, and Eleanor laughed again, putting her hand on his arm and looking up into his eyes.

It was a sweet moment, but it made Peter uncomfortable. Not in a they're being too affectionate kind of way. But more a

I wish I had someone to look at me like that kind of way.

He looked away.

"I think you'll want to come. I think you'll have a good time, and there's going to be good food there. Which is why I'm going," Eleanor said, bringing him back to the subject they were talking about.

He looked over at the wide expanse of blue sky and the slice of lake they could see around the edge of the inn. He loved his town, happy that God had seen fit to move both him and Franklin to Strawberry Sands. It had been a good move. But he didn't want to be matched up with just anyone. And he had a hunch that if he went tonight, Norma Jean would be trying to figure out how she could trap him again.

"I understand there's going to be dancing," Franklin said, as though that would convince him.

"Yeah. Sally told me there was going to be, and if Norma Jean is in the band, she'll be providing music, and... Sally will probably be looking for a partner since she usually hangs out with Norma Jean at those things, but since Norma Jean's going to be busy playing, Sally would probably appreciate having someone to hang out with."

Well, of course that made Peter's ears perk up. If Norma Jean was in the band, she wouldn't be chasing him around the floor, trying to get a hold of him and take him off somewhere.

Sally. You could be dancing with her.

"All right. Maybe I'll go."

Chapter 3

Peter was glad that he agreed to go as he looked around at the sparkling lights that stretched the whole way from the boardwalk to the water.

Lake Michigan didn't have major tides like the ocean, but there was a little bit of play involved in where the water hit the sand, and the poles for the lights were currently being lapped by the waves.

It was beautiful. Whoever had planned it had a vision that Peter could only dream about.

Normally he didn't take off work much. The farm kept him busy, but he supposed he could be lured out for certain things. One of those things was Sally.

She sat over beside the punch table, sipping from a plastic cup and talking to Miss Lana. He didn't want to go over and interrupt their conversation but had been standing along the edge, waiting for Miss Lana to walk away.

He'd been waiting for twenty minutes.

Thankfully, he could still see Norma Jean sitting on the bandstand, holding her trombone. She'd only hit one person with it that evening as far as he could tell, and Peter was pretty sure that was an accident.

Sally, on the other hand, had been talking to a group of girls when he arrived and had instructed them on how to dance, even though she mostly had to hop around on one foot. He appreciated her cheerful spirits and loved that she was good with children too.

Not for the first time, he wondered what someone like her was doing with Norma Jean.

Regardless, Lana walked away, and Peter took a deep breath. This was his opportunity. If he didn't ask her soon, he would miss his opportunity. He didn't want to stand around and end up dancing with a bunch of people he wasn't interested in. Plus, he had to get up early in the morning to take care of his animals and didn't want to be out too late.

He strode across the floor, keeping his eye on Sally, who continued to sit on the folding chair by the table, sipping her drink, her eyes roving over the crowd as though she were checking to make sure that everyone had a dancing partner.

She was so serious, so considerate, and he was such a goofball. He couldn't imagine that she would be interested in someone like him, but he wouldn't know unless he tried. So, he forced himself to finish walking over.

When he was about three feet away, Sally's eyes swept the crowd again, and she saw him coming.

Her eyes widened, and her mouth opened. She didn't get anything out before he closed the distance between them and spoke.

"It's a nice evening. Your lights work just fine. They're pretty."

"Thanks, I'm glad we took the time to do it." She frowned and looked around like she was looking for an escape. When she didn't find one, she looked back at him. "You don't usually come to these things."

"I thought this was the first beach bash to celebrate the end of summer in Strawberry Sands," he said, giving it its full title and description, although he didn't know why. Maybe just to get more words in or to get his mouth warmed up. He wasn't sure. Normally he didn't have to do that. Conversations came easily to him, and he was considered quite funny.

"It is, but I meant I don't usually see you around town at any events we have. Like the Strawberry Sands Festival or the Strawberry Valentine's Day extravaganza."

"I think on Valentine's Day, I was busy thawing the water that had frozen on Valentine's Day eve."

"Oh. I guess it's important that your animals have water to drink."

"Yeah. I thought that was a little more important than showing up for the party in town, although I heard there was a lot of chocolate here, and I was kind of sad I missed it."

"I'm sorry. Franklin should have made sure you got some of the leftovers. There was plenty."

"I'll have to put a bug in his ear for next year. Unless... Unless I make it." He wanted to say unless he had a woman who could do that for him, but woman didn't sound right, and girl sounded not right either, and he didn't want to say girlfriend, because he really preferred wife, although the idea of being married less than six months from that day was a little bit...scary, but at the same time, he didn't mind it. Really. Especially as he stood and looked at Sally, with her no-nonsense haircut and her sweet smile.

"I was kind of hoping you might want to dance." There. He said it.

But to his surprise, her cheeks started to get red. He didn't understand it and tried to figure out what in the world was going on.

"Well, I suppose that's the reason I'm sitting down."

"Because I was going to come over and ask you to dance?"

"No. Because you were right earlier today when Norma Jean fell off the ladder. I twisted my foot, and while I don't think it's a serious injury, it hurts."

"I knew it. Why weren't you honest about it? You told me it didn't hurt."

Sally bit her lip, and again her gaze slid sideways, toward the band. Maybe she was looking at Norma Jean. Finally, she lowered her voice so that he had to lean forward to hear her. "I didn't want to take any attention away from Norma Jean."

"Why not?" He didn't understand that.

"Because... Because I knew it would upset her."

"She always has to be the center of attention?"

"Well, I know that sounds terrible, and I don't mean for it to. Norma Jean is my best friend, and I love her. I don't want to say anything unkind about her."

"Isn't it okay to speak the truth?"

"We're supposed to speak the truth in love. And I think sometimes it's better to say nothing rather than say the truth which could be hurtful."

He couldn't argue with that, and he appreciated the fact that that's how she felt. Still, he felt like she was allowing Norma Jean and what she wanted to influence her life a little bit more than what was necessary.

"So if Norma Jean weren't here, you'd have gone to the diner with me?"

She looked down and fiddled with her cup that sat on the table.

"Maybe," she finally said. He felt like that was the truth.

"What would I have to do to talk you into it?" He clamped down on his tongue. He didn't want to have to talk some girl into wanting to be with him. Except, he kinda felt that if he had a little bit more time to spend with Sally, he could loosen up and be himself, and she would enjoy being with him. If he could only talk her into it.

"Nothing. I... I just have this thing where if my friend is interested in someone, then I step back. I don't usually have that problem." She chuckled. "In case you haven't noticed, Norma Jean is gorgeous. But regardless, if she has a preference, I just allow her to move forward, and I don't. I'm sure she would do the same for me."

She didn't say that with a whole lot of conviction, and Peter got the feeling that perhaps there had been more than one time in their relationship when Norma Jean had taken a man that Sally had been interested in. Sally didn't say anything more though, and Peter couldn't fault her for her values. He appreciated someone who cared about their friend enough that they wouldn't step on any toes.

"What if I say I'm not interested in her? Does that change anything?" He was pretty sure it would. After all, if there was no chance for Norma Jean and him to have anything, there was no need for Sally to stand back.

"Not really. I have to wait until Norma Jean decides she's not interested."

"Well, she's playing in the band right now."

The band had stopped for just a moment, finishing one song, and then they went into an introduction for the next.

"I love that song," Sally said with a smile as she set her chin on her hand and listened.

"Come on, we don't have to do anything more than stand and sway." He didn't think she was going to take him up on it, and he really wasn't sure he wanted her to. She said her foot wasn't hurt that bad, but she had told him already that she wasn't hurt at all, so he wasn't sure he believed her. He thought maybe she was one of those people that down-played anything that was wrong with themself in order to focus attention on other people. And he supposed that was something a caregiver had a tendency to do. He'd heard that she'd been a care-giver for her aunt until her death earlier that year.

"I really do love this song... Okay," she said, shoving her chair back and stand-ing to her feet. Or her foot, since she had one foot up.

Stepping forward, he put his arm around her on the side of her hurt foot.

"You can lean on me," he said, thinking maybe it wasn't a bad thing that she had hurt her foot.

"Thank you," she said as she hopped around the table, putting weight on him as he steadied and balanced her.

"We can just stand here. We don't have to go too far."

"Thank you. It's...a little bit hard to sit and watch while everyone else has fun."

"It's hard to watch you sit when I'd rather be dancing with you," he said in return. That made her smile, and that gave him a little bit of confidence.

Although, he didn't feel the need to speak when she stepped in his arms, and he wrapped them around her, pulling her close. True to his word, he didn't move, but planted his feet, and just swayed from side to side.

She hummed a little to the music, and he enjoyed listening to her.

"You must really like the song. You seem to know all the words."

"Yeah, it was one of my favorites growing up. I have always loved music, and I'm a little jealous of people who can play an instrument."

"If you were playing an instrument, you wouldn't be able to dance," he pointed out reasonably.

She laughed, looking up at him, her face just barely an inch from his. "That's a good point. Are you always so pragmatic?"

"No. Usually I'm…known as the goofy one. But when you have a brother like mine, it doesn't really take much to be known as someone who's never serious, since he's never not serious."

"Eleanor seems very happy with him."

"She does. Sometimes I wonder how that can be, but I suppose you can't explain love."

"I guess you can't," she said, and he forgot to sway. Somehow he was caught in her eyes, and maybe it was the festive atmosphere, the end of summer, the last glimmer of the sunset on the lake, the twinkling lights above them that could almost be stars, or maybe it was just Sally. He wasn't sure what it was, but the swaying stopped, and he slowly lowered his head.

Was he really going to kiss her? He could hardly believe it; that hadn't been his intention. He wanted to come over and talk to her. Kissing really hadn't been on his agenda, but he couldn't seem to stop the movement of his head as it continued down. Maybe if there had been some sign from her that she hadn't wanted him to continue, he would have stopped. But her gaze turned dreamy, and then her eyes slowly closed. As she lifted her head, meeting his.

He forgot about the music, forgot about the people on the floor, forgot that he was supposed to be dancing, and even forgot that the woman he was about to kiss had a sore foot. He forgot everything but the feel of his arms around her, the feel of her warmth under his hands, and her breath as it fanned across his face. Her scent, sweet and a little minty, as she stood before him. There was a soft touch of fruit, maybe strawberries, and a feeling that settled deep inside of him that this was exactly right.

From somewhere that seemed like it was far, far away from him, he realized that the music had stopped, after someone had hit a very bad note. He didn't pay any attention, but then a voice called out, "Sally Marianne Curtis! What in the world do you think you're doing?" And Sally jerked back from him, putting weight on her sore foot, which caused her to stumble.

He reached forward to grab hold of her to help her stand, but she stumbled even more as she struggled to get away from him.

Just a few seconds before, she had been content, leaning into him, holding on tight, and now she didn't seem to be able to stand his touch.

What had he done?

Except he knew. It was Norma Jean who had just yelled at her best friend, and that was what Sally had been telling him, that she would stand back because of Norma Jean. So that must be what made her struggle to get away from him.

"Let me help you to your seat," he said, and his words sounded irritated, even to him.

That was mostly because he was irritated. Not at Sally. At Norma Jean.

"Please don't touch me," Sally said, sounding a little breathless, although he doubted it was from their near kiss. It was probably more because of the pain in her foot.

He lifted his hands up in the air, like he was showing that he didn't have a weapon, rather than holding his hands away so she wouldn't feel the need to struggle anymore. It was just a second after that that she grimaced, and Norma Jean arrived, panting, at their side.

"What kind of friend are you? You know that Peter is mine. I saw him first, I called it. How dare you step in and try to steal him out from underneath me!"

"Sally wasn't doing anything. I asked her to dance."

"You stay out of this," Norma Jean said, pointing a glossy purple fingernail right in his nose.

He took a step back without even thinking about it. That fingernail could double as a weapon.

"Don't yell at him. It was all my fault. I… I shouldn't have been dancing. My foot hurts."

"Yeah, you've been sobbing about your poor foot since dinnertime today. I think it was to get out of work." Norma Jean put her nose in the air. "Why don't you just go on home. At least get out of my sight. I can hardly stand to look at you. Some friend you are."

Hurt crossed Sally's face, then she lifted her chin.

"Sorry," she said, although she didn't sound like she was begging. She sounded like she was stating a fact. And Peter had no trouble believing that she truly was sorry.

Kind of made him sorry that he'd insisted that they needed to dance, because he hadn't realized how much it would upset Sally to have Norma Jean upset at her.

He supposed Sally was a kind person who liked for everyone to get along. He was that kind of person too, although people like Norma Jean irritated him. He'd like to tell her a thing or two, but he supposed that wasn't really his job.

Sally had mentioned it a little bit earlier, saying that it was just her job to love her.

He knew God put people like that in a person's life to rub off their own rough edges. It was up to each individual to fix themselves according to Scripture, and it was not for him to criticize or be unkind to Norma Jean.

Still, he couldn't consider someone like Norma Jean a friend. Not for him.

Maybe there was more to her than met the eye.

Regardless, he watched as Sally gave Norma Jean a glance, and Norma Jean jutted her chin out. Sally grabbed the crutch he hadn't seen lying across the chair beside her and, without looking at him, limped slowly away from the table and toward the sidewalk.

"Now, if you want to dance, I'd love for you to dance with me," Norma Jean said, giving him a sultry smile and putting one hand on his shoulder.

"Nah. I think I'm done dancing for the night. It's time for me to go home. I need to get up pretty early in the morning to feed the stock."

"Wait a minute. If you have time to dance with her, you can dance with me too."

"I thought you were mad at me? Weren't you not talking to me?"

"I decided to forgive you. Although, I'm going to change my mind if you don't give me this dance," Norma Jean insisted as what was left of the band started up another tune.

The talking on the beach had stopped, as everyone had been watching the scene before them, but as the band started up, people started moving and chattering again.

Still, Peter had lost his taste for any kind of entertainment. He didn't want to hate Norma Jean, because Sally obvious-ly didn't, but he didn't have to like her. And he definitely didn't have to dance with her.

"Thanks for considering me, but I'll pass." He turned around and walked away. Although he could hear Norma Jean saying something, he didn't stop to try to figure out what it was. For once, he was glad that the music drowned out the sound of someone trying to speak with him.

Sally was already out of sight, and Peter left without even taking a piece of Griff's strawberry cream cheese cobbler. Which, in his mind, showed exactly how upset he was.

Chapter 4

"You know, Mom, now that all of your children are married, do you think it's time for you to find someone?"

Lana laughed a little, as she straightened the cookie trays on the table. Sunday meant well, but she didn't understand what it was like to be in her mid-fifties, already married and divorced once, already have a family, and not know how to fit into someone else's family. When a person was young, they had their whole future ahead of them, and they were looking for someone to share it with, for someone to build something with.

Lana had already built her life. And men her age had already built theirs, too. Trying to meld two lives that were already in place together somehow... She just didn't know if she would be able to do it. Or if she could find someone with whom she would want to put that kind of effort into.

The whole thing just seemed... Depressing.

"Aren't you lonely sometimes, Mom?" Sunday asked, putting a hand on Lana's arm so her hand stilled on the last cookie tray.

The lights sparkled, the breeze off the lake was warm, although it had cooled since the sun went down. Happy laughter trailed over the evening air, and she felt safe and content, surrounded by friends and neighbors and family. People she loved.

"Sometimes. But, God is really going to have to be clear if he wants me to find someone else." She wasn't going to just jump into a relationship because she was lonely. There was a lot more to it than that. When she was younger she would have had decades to spend with someone as they worked to allow their relationship to become a picture of Christ and the church, as God intended according to the Bible.

But now? She had so much baggage, and she couldn't imagine meeting a man who didn't have baggage as well. If he didn't, what kind of life would he have had?

Or maybe it was fear. Fear she wouldn't be able to live up to the memories of a first wife. Whether she had died, or whether he was divorced. She supposed there was definitely fear involved.

"Just don't close your eyes to the possibility," Sunday advised her, patting her arm. "I'd feel a lot better if I felt like you were happy."

"I am happy." She was. Usually. What more could a woman want than to have her children surrounding her, happily married, with spouses that God had chosen, and with grandchildren growing up near her home, lots of family get-togethers, and in the community that she loved and felt like she was a part of?

She did long for a relationship with someone, sure. Someone who cherished her, knew what she was like deep down inside and loved her anyway. Someone to snuggle with at night, someone to hold her hand, someone to walk through the most difficult time of her life so far, old age.

"It looks like my husband wants to dance," Sunday said, happiness and excitement in her voice. "Don't forget what I said, okay?"

"If God is clear, I'll do what He wants," was the only promise that Lana would make. Anything else just seemed like it was too hard.

She smiled as Sunday hurried off, embracing her husband, and stepping into his arms with the familiarity of one who knew she was loved and who loved in return.

It made Lana's heart happy to see her daughter was with someone who cared so much about her.

She finished straightening the cookie trays, and then stood up, looking over the dance floor at the couples who were slow dancing.

Over on the far side, her eyes caught on something that she wasn't expecting, and she moved back, squinting to look a little closer.

Pierre? Yes, she was sure that was Pierre, the son of the man she had been visiting for several years now at the lighthouse up the beach.

Pierre was not alone.

As she watched, three small children stayed close to his legs - a little girl held tightly to his hand, while two boys pressed against each side.

She remembered the one and only time she'd spoken with him. She'd been so out of character, being so brazen as to suggest that he do something meaningful with his life. She never talked like that to strangers, and never to acquaintances or family of people she considered friends.

But, all that aside, could it be that Pierre took her seriously?

As far as she knew he just had an adult daughter and that daughter did not have any children.

As he moved, she looked around for Joe, his father, but she did not see him.

Was it possible that Pierre had come to the Beach Bash at Strawberry Sands with...foster children?

Straightening her spine, she moved around the edge of the dance floor, careful to stay out of the couples' way, and made her way over to Pierre, whose eyes roved over the dance floor, as though he was looking for someone.

"Pierre! I wasn't expecting to see you tonight. But I'm glad you're here," she said, unable to keep the surprise out of her tone.

But she gave the children a benevolent smile. "And you brought some friends."

"These are my foster kids," Pierre said, and while the words were simple, there was a message in his eyes that Lana couldn't miss. He had the children because of her.

She didn't think for one second that she had that much influence over anyone, and for a few moments she was speechless.

"You listened to me."

"You made sense."

She'd said something about not wasting his life. About living for something higher than himself. About how he was doing everything he did to make himself more comfortable, looking forward to his free time so he could spend it making himself happy.

"I'm sorry. I regretted that conversation for a long time. I still regret it."

"Don't. I think that conversation changed my life. It definitely made me realize a few things." Their eyes met and held, and then, he broke eye contact and smiled a little, indicating the children around him.

"Let me introduce you to my foster children," he said, patting the little girl on the head, before indicating the two boys.

He rattled off their names, and Lana listened, but the whole time she felt convicted about herself. She had suggested that he do something with his life, and immediately he had gone and done something. Something meaningful, something sacrificial, something not the least bit selfish or self-centered. And yet there she was; she hadn't changed a thing.

Part of her argued that she was already doing a lot of things to serve and help other people, but if he could improve, couldn't she?

"It's so nice to meet you. Did you guys get some cookies to eat?"

They shook their heads, so sweet and endearing, and she looked back at Pierre. "Can I take you to the food tables?"

"I would love it if you would," Pierre said..

She led them over to the food tables, and helped all the children grab plates and fill them with their selections from the different offerings. They found seats at the picnic tables that were set up around the perimeter of the dance floor, and Pierre invited her to sit while they ate.

She declined, although she wanted to accept.

Pierre had impressed her beyond words. Impressed her with how he had put action and time and sacrifice behind his words and made a real life change, rather than just giving it a bunch of lip service, and then continuing to do whatever he wanted.

Throughout the evening she kept an eye on the small family, noticing that several of her daughters and other town members went over to welcome them. At one point, the children got up and joined in the organized games that the entertainment committee had come up with.

Pierre disappeared, and Lana busied herself making sure the punch bowl stayed filled up and the cookie trays were never empty.

"Would you dance with me?" a voice said from behind her as she retied a stray balloon to a light pole.

"Oh my goodness. You scared me," she said, turning and putting her hand to her chest, and speaking more to give herself a moment to think than because she was so startled.

It was Pierre, and he was asking her to dance.

He wasn't playing fair.

"I'm sorry. I just... I've been waiting for a chance, and right now my kids are playing games with the other children. I asked the girl in charge of the games if she would keep an eye on them so I could have one dance. She seemed happy to do that," he said with a smile. "And so I'm here. Spending my one dance on you if you'll have me."

"Of course I'll have you," she said, putting her hand in his outstretched palm, trying to ignore the fact that her throat was suddenly dry and his hand felt warm and strong and seemed to fit with hers perfectly.

"Thank you," he said, leading her to the dance floor.

She gave herself a little lecture on the way. Reminding herself that she was a half-century old, and was too old to have silly schoolgirl dreams. The kind of dreams that Pierre seemed to incite in her. The rest of the time she tried to think of questions she could ask him to keep the conversation going, so she could try to hide the fact that she was really looking forward to dancing with him.

He stopped at the edge of the floor, turned, put an arm around her waist while holding her other hand in his.

She put a hand on his shoulder and fell into step with him. They moved easily together, not perfectly, but just like her hand in his had felt right, moving across from him felt right as well.

"After I spoke with you, I realize that you were right. That I had raised a daughter, and I felt like I deserved a break from children, and I liked that my life was orderly and perfect, and I didn't realize that I never stopped to think that there was a lot of suffering in the world, and I could do something to alleviate it. It's easy to sit in my comfortable chair in my comfortable office and expect someone else to do something, while I maybe scroll social media and like a few posts and talk about how someone should be doing something, or criticizing people who are doing things, but never thinking that maybe I should take action."

"That's a big lie from social media. We feel like we've done something if we press the like button and leave an encouraging comment."

"And that's not nothing. But, I can be doing far more. I just...was selfish."

"We're all selfish." She didn't want him to think that she thought she wasn't. "So you ended up with three children?"

"I had three spare bedrooms. I've got a big empty apartment, and no one in it."

"And now there is someone. Lots of someones."

"Kind of funny how quickly you can fall in love with them. I'm not saying that everything is easy."

"I was wondering about it, but I didn't want to ask and make you feel like you need to talk about it if you didn't want to."

"It's been quite an adjustment. But, I can tell already that I've grown, and hopefully will continue to do so. It's opened up a lot of doors for me, and...I'm thinking pretty strongly about adopting them."

"Adopting three children?"

"Crazy, isn't it? And I'm fifty-five. That almost seems too old."

"I think it's only too old if we let it be," Lana said, thinking he wasn't much older than she was.

"I guess I would be thinking more seriously about it if I had a wife. It seems... Almost like I'm not helping the children if they go from a bad home, to the home of a single man."

"Children need a mom," she said automatically. But, then she added, "And a dad."

"Both," he said with conviction.

"I raised my children without a father for the most part, and I think sometimes the Lord can fill in the gap if we depend on

Him. I'm not saying it's easy or that it's best, just saying He can."

"And sometimes He gives us an actual person to fill in the gap with us."

At that, Pierre stopped moving, and he put both hands on her shoulders. They were at the edge of the dance floor, so Lana supposed no one noticed, although she couldn't say whether they did or not because she couldn't look away from the intense seriousness of his eyes. "I know we don't know each other very well, but you have a pretty good relationship with my father, and he can tell you what kind of man I am. I won't have time to court you like you deserve, but... If you're interested in filling the position of mom for these kids, I feel like we could make it work."

Lana blinked. Was he saying what she thought he was?

She had never thought that she might be in a position like this, but if she had, she wasn't expecting the reaction of her emotions. It wasn't excitement, it wasn't even flattery. It wasn't offense over what she was fairly sure was an off-hand offer of marriage.

It was fear. Deep and strong and sharp, it sliced up her inside and ballooned throughout her chest.

"Mr. Pierre! Mr. Pierre!" Three little bodies hurled themselves at Pierre, shattering the spell that might have wrapped around them, and allowing Lana to take a step back, breaking contact, as her hand fell from his shoulder and his slid from her waist and their clasped hands loosened.

"The lady said we could take a carriage ride if you would come with us! Please!"

"Oh! They started carriage rides. How nice. It's a lovely night for it and so pretty and it's not too cold. I think your children would love it."

"You could come," Pierre said, but his words just made the panic that was bubbling inside her more caustic.

"No. No. I wouldn't want to get in the way of a good family thing."

"You wouldn't be."

"Please! Can we go now? They said we could go first!"

"Sure," Pierre said, although his eyes were still holding Lana's. She shook her head, backing away, her hand at her throat. She wasn't ready to just jump into a marriage. She was going to be choosy. She would make sure that if she did do marriage a second time, it wasn't going to be a spur of the moment decision where some man needed a mother for his children so she hopped into the position like the marriage wasn't a lifetime commitment, and like she hadn't been cheated on and betrayed and cast aside and abandoned once already.

Once was enough in a lifetime.

"Are you sure?" Pierre asked softly over the chatter of the children around him.

He had gone and done something brave. Something that Lana herself had wanted to do, but just hadn't. And now, he was asking her to do something brave too. Something selfless. Something that could potentially change four lives. But she shook her head no. And then, she couldn't watch as Pierre, holding the hand of the little girl, his arm around the shoulders of one of the boys, turned and walked away, his children at his side.

That's the kind of man she wished she would have married to begin with. But it was too late. Wasn't it?

Chapter 5

Sally listened to her GPS tell her to turn left at Strawberry Farm Road. She could see the road coming up and put on her turn signal.

As she did, she smiled a little at the memories. The shed that she had accidentally locked Franklin in was just up the road a piece. She had been horrified and totally uncertain what to do.

Doing that kind of thing was so far out of her normal, she panicked.

But it had all worked for the best, since Eleanor had gone to rescue him, had ended up stranded with him, and now they were happily married.

Sally could almost be proud of herself, since she had hooked her friend up with her husband, and even though that night she had been beside herself with embarrassment, she was happy for them now and loved it when they gave her credit for their relationship.

Turning onto Strawberry Farm Road, she glanced at the ETA. Two minutes.

She had never been down the road to the actual farmhouse, although she knew it was back there somewhere. She wasn't going there today and probably never would, since Peter lived there.

He had to hate her for the way she treated him two weeks ago at the End of Summer Beach Bash.

She hadn't wanted to embarrass him in front of everyone, but that was probably what happened when a man asked a woman to dance and she couldn't get away from him fast enough.

Norma Jean had been mad at her until yesterday when they finally made up.

Norma Jean had some issues in her past that Sally tried to give her leniency for. A person's upbringing didn't give them license to be unkind. At least it shouldn't, but Sally did try to show grace to Norma Jean, because Norma Jean hadn't had all the advantages that Sally had in her life.

Perhaps if Sally had been raised the way Norma Jean had, she would have ended up the same way.

She didn't really know, but she liked to think that she could be considerate and kind, even when she didn't feel like it, which honestly, after Norma Jean had interrupted Peter almost kissing her, she had to search pretty deep in order to find the kindness that usually came a lot easier to her. Regardless, she tried to put that from her head and focus on the new job she was going to.

Franklin had told her it was down the same road as the farm, and that she would be going to a small office that would be about half a mile up the road.

He hadn't told her anything about the business, and she got the feeling that he didn't know much. Although she remembered the way Eleanor kind of smiled while Franklin had been talking to her, and it made her wonder if there was something they weren't telling her.

Regardless, she was going to be working very near Peter's farm, and that was something she hadn't told Norma Jean.

Norma Jean had forgiven her, but Sally knew it wouldn't take much to upset her again.

She tried to shove all that out of her mind and focus on the job at hand. Franklin had told her she was going to be dealing with accounting books that were very messed up, and she could expect to spend a good bit of time untangling them.

Sally could have rubbed her hands together in anticipation. This was where she was in her element. Figuring things out, making the numbers make sense, manipulating them and moving them, straightening up the lines and making everything look nice and neat.

She couldn't wait to get started. This was the perfect thing to keep her occupied over the winter. And it wasn't a terrible drive out, so if they did get snow, she would be able to make it anyway.

That was important, since if she had to get a job at Blueberry Beach or even further south toward Chicago, winter weather could make the commute miserable. She felt very blessed to be working so close to home.

The GPS rattled off the address and then said, "You have arrived at your destination."

Sally smiled, parking her car, looking at the cute little building that had a sign that said Office hanging on the green door. The building was painted white, and there were lots of big windows. So many that she could see the whole way through the building from the front window to the back.

That was one thing she hated about working inside—sometimes it felt like she didn't get to see the sky all day long. This would be a beautiful place to work.

She looked around a little as she got out of the car, wondering exactly where Peter's farm was. She really didn't have a clue, and she didn't want to ask. After the debacle with Norma Jean, she didn't want to think about Peter at all.

Although, at night, after she went to bed, she allowed herself to snuggle up to the memory of "dancing" with Peter. They hadn't really danced much. Just swayed to the music because of her ankle. Then, he lowered his head, and she'd pictured it a thousand times. But only in the safety of her bedroom at night. Nowhere Norma Jean could ever get wind of it.

Tucking those thoughts away, she straightened her back, put her purse over her shoulder, and walked with purpose to the little door, rapping sharply on it. She tried to project an aurora of competence and professionalism.

She wasn't sure she'd say she was successful, but she did know that her facade crumbled as soon as the door opened, because Peter stood on the other side of it.

Her mouth hung open, and her heart stopped and then started again, beating as fast as though she had just run a mile.

Of course. That's why Eleanor had been smiling. That's why she had wondered if she had been missing something. Because they had deliberately not told her that she was going out to Peter's farm, not near it, on it, in order to get this job.

She really needed the job, although as she stood there, her mouth flopping up and down like a fish out of water, she tried to figure out if she could afford to turn around and walk away.

The hours at the inn would be dwindling, as tourist season was over, and while she wasn't in danger of losing her apartment, she didn't want to get to that point either.

She liked to be able to eat as well, and yeah, she wasn't going to be proud about this.

The one thing that helped make up her mind was that Peter seemed just as shocked to see her as she was to see him.

His brother had sent Sally.

Peter stood staring in shock at the woman who stood before him. Sally.

He thought about her a lot in the last two weeks. Wondered how her ankle was doing, wishing that he'd been a little faster and had been able to catch her, or faster that evening and had actually kissed her before they got interrupted. Except, that didn't seem right, because he didn't want to rush his first kiss with

Sally. He wanted it to be the first of many. He wanted her to enjoy it and not feel like he was taking something that she wasn't sure she wanted to give him.

Regardless, it was all hindsight now, because it was done and over with. He hadn't caught her, hadn't gotten the kiss, and he hadn't gotten to talk to her again.

At least if he were doing it over, he would have gotten her phone number. Except, he was pretty sure that she wasn't going to talk to him, because Norma Jean hadn't given up her pursuit.

"Hello. You must be the accountant that Franklin said was going to be showing up at my door any moment."

"Yeah, I am. He neglected to mention that I was coming to your farm. He said it was near your farm."

"Well, to be completely accurate, the farm is on down the road another half mile, on the right. That's where the house and barns are."

"Interesting. I would have thought that the office would be right by the farm."

"I don't know that this was originally an office, but it seemed like a good place to put one. The building was already here. I think it might have been a fruit stand at one time."

"I love the big windows. They struck me right away."

"I really like them too. I love to be outside, and when I have to be in here doing paperwork, it helps that the windows let in a lot of sunlight, so I don't always feel like I'm stuck inside."

He couldn't quite read the expression on her face, kind of a half-smile, half-thoughtful look. But it didn't really matter, because he was going to get to spend a long time with Sally. He could kiss his brother's cheek right now.

And here he was concerned about the tangle that he'd gotten his books into, but now he wished it was even more convoluted, because that would mean more time with Sally. Maybe he could find more things for her to do.

"Are you looking for a full-time job?" he asked, hoping he didn't wait too long to speak, but she seemed enraptured with his windows and pleased with the general look of the office. It wasn't spartan, but he didn't have it cluttered up with a lot of things.

"Not really. I'm still working at the inn, but you know how it is in the winter. When the tourists leave, everything slows down."

"Maybe I'll be able to lure you away."

She just smiled and didn't say that was possible, but she also didn't say that she would never leave the inn, which he felt was a good thing.

Maybe he had been so enraptured with talking to Sally, or maybe even thinking so much about all the excuses he could use to spend more time in the office that he didn't hear the car pulling in, because he was totally shocked when the door burst open.

"I'm here about the accountant job!" Norma Jean said as she strode in, shutting the door behind her and walking until she stood just slightly in front of Sally.

She barely glanced at her friend but looked at Peter like he held the only life vest on a sinking ship.

"I'm sorry, but the position has been—"

"You can have it," Sally said, interrupting him and turning to face her friend.

"You were here first." He felt like it was his choice who got the job, but both women ignored him.

"But I want it!" Norma Jean said, stomping her foot. "I mean, I need it! I'm depending on this job. You have to give it to me."

"Of course. You can have it," Sally said, and he wanted to grab her by the neck. Not in a strangling her kind of way, but in a what are you thinking about kind of way. How could she just give the job that she was here for, and she needed, to her friend? Using the word loosely since he didn't really see Norma Jean as being a very good friend to Sally.

"All right. Then it's settled. See you later, Sally," Norma Jean said, waving a few fingers at Sally, before she turned back to him. "Are you going to show me what I need to do?"

He blinked; things had happened too fast for him to keep up. "Sally. The job is yours."

"I don't want it anymore. Thank you anyway. I appreciate your time. I know Norma Jean will do a good job. Truly. She's a great worker and dependable too." She smiled at her friend, and Peter didn't get it. How could she be so kind to someone who didn't treat her well at all?

"Thanks, Sally," Norma Jean said, and there seemed to be a softening around her eyes, or maybe her shoulders weren't quite as stiff as though she hadn't been sure whether Sally was going to fight her about the job or not. There was an interesting dynamic going on there, and Peter couldn't figure it out. All he knew was that he wanted Sally in the office with him, and he didn't want to be stuck in the office with Norma Jean.

Sally smiled and gave him a more serious look, one which he didn't understand what it meant, and then she opened the door and slipped out.

He wanted to smack his head against the wall. He had been so close. Franklin had basically given him a gift, dropping it right in his lap, and Norma Jean had come and snatched it away from him, although he could hardly fault Norma Jean when Sally could have had the job.

She'd just allowed Norma Jean to take it from her. Without even fighting for it.

There was a part of him that felt depressed, low, and sad, because Sally apparently didn't think that he was worth fighting for. He wanted her to want to be with him. And it was discouraging that she obviously didn't, although she did seem to like him.

He was never very good at this type of thing, and he supposed he should just let it go. He really, really liked Sally. His eyes were drawn to her every time they were in the same room, and the idea of being around her filled him with excitement, and she was a good person. Kind, generous, loyal to a fault to her friends, and the kind of woman that once she gave her loyalty to him, she would never take it away. He wanted a wife like that. But it seemed like whenever he was around, Norma Jean was there too, and she had Sally's first loyalty.

He had no idea how to earn that for himself.

He should allow Sally to be an example for him, he figured as he turned back to Norma Jean. She was kind to Norma Jean, even when Norma Jean wasn't exceptionally nice to Sally. If Peter wanted to earn Sally's loyalty, the very least he could do would be to try to up his game in that area. He found Norma Jean distasteful, mostly because she kept trying to come between Sally and him and kept chasing him even when he felt like he'd been clear about not being interested. But Sally had a lot more beef with Norma Jean, and she'd been nice.

Taking a breath, he tried to put a pleasant look on his face as he turned toward Norma Jean. "I guess if it's okay with you, you're my new accountant."

"Oh, it's more than okay. And I'm really good at this too. Just show me your books, and I'll work my magic." She wrinkled her nose and winked an eye, and Peter wanted to back out rather than move forward, but he just motioned and began to show her all the things that he had been planning on showing his new accountant until he had gotten distracted by Sally's unexpected appearance.

This wasn't what he planned, but maybe it was just the Lord saying that he needed to learn to be nice to people. Or maybe it was just the Lord saying that he needed to learn to be nice to people while he was becoming more patient and waiting on the things that were going to happen. Because he might learn to like Norma Jean, but there was never going to be anything more between them. Maybe he would have an opportunity to let her know.

Chapter 7

Sally sat by the lake, contemplating what she had just done. She had given up the accountant position that, first of all, she needed and, second of all, would have brought her into daily contact with Peter, whom she admired and respected and would like to have gotten to know better, except Norma Jean had claimed him first.

Was she taking the friend thing too far? After all, wasn't it a commonly established protocol that if a person's friend put a claim on a man, then there was nothing she could do until that friend gave up the claim?

She wasn't exactly sure how it went, because it never applied to her before. She just knew she was depressed and sad. She felt like she'd lost something that she'd never really had but always wanted. Plus, she needed a job. Working at the inn all winter wasn't going to provide enough money for her to continue to pay her bills.

She wasn't going to go under right away, but it would be soon if she didn't figure something out.

"Hello. I didn't realize you were down here," Lana said as she walked up to her. "Is it okay if I sit a spell?"

"Sure," Sally said, trying to put a happy smile on her face but knowing she failed.

"It's a pretty day. We need to enjoy this weather while it lasts. Pretty soon, it's going to be cold and... I want to say miserable, but there is a certain beauty about winter that I just love."

"Me too. I get tired of it though. A lot faster than I get tired of the hot weather."

"I'm the same. I can handle being hot a lot better than I can handle being cold, but I think it's the darkness that really gets to me," Lana said as she settled into the sand beside Sally, stretching her legs out and leaning back on her hands.

"Yeah, I don't know. I guess it's just such a long time where you're kind of not stuck inside exactly, but not a whole lot of people are out and about. I do my best thinking outside. It's kind of hard to think outside when you're freezing to death." Sally laughed a little, and Lana's warm chuckle drifted into the air right alongside her. There was just something about Lana that made a person feel safe and happy and like she was a motherly figure to them.

Sally figured she couldn't be the only person like that, but since her parents were split up, and neither one of them really seemed to care too much about her, it was nice to have someone who did.

"I hope I'm not bothering you," Lana said as she settled down and lifted her head to the breeze.

"Not at all. I appreciate you seeing me and coming over. I... I guess I feel like maybe I did something that I shouldn't have."

"You want to talk about it?" Lana asked easily, and Sally seemed to read in her tone that Lana didn't care if Sally wanted to keep it to herself or if she wanted to speak. She was welcome to do either, and that made her feel like she was free to say what she wanted to.

"I want to be a loyal friend, but some-times... I'm not sure if I'm just a little bit too loyal?"

That wasn't exactly what she wanted to say, but she couldn't think of the words to get anything else out.

"I don't think there's any such thing as too loyal. It's always good to know your convictions and stick to them. Whether it's being a good friend or being a good daughter or wife or even a fan of a sports team." Lana chuckled. "Not that I know anything about that."

Sally laughed. She couldn't imagine Miss Lana cheering for a sports team. She was always busy doing something or helping people, and that just didn't seem like something Miss Lana would stop to do.

"But if you want to talk about it, I'll listen."

"It's about Norma Jean."

"You've been a good friend to her."

"Yeah." Sally didn't want to go into Norma Jean's history. Not that she thought that would change the way Miss Lana treated her, she just...didn't want to get into it.

"I tried to set Norma Jean up with Peter. You know, Franklin's brother."

"Yeah. He's a nice fellow. Funny, and a little bit goofy, especially when he's next to his brother. But I've heard he's a hard worker and he's doing his best to make a profit out there on that farm of his."

"Yeah, well, he needed an accountant." She stopped. "But I'm getting ahead of myself."

"I'm sorry. I interrupted you. Just keep talking, and ignore me."

"It's okay. You can interrupt me any-time. I just... I thought Peter and Norma Jean would be good together, and Norma Jean seems to have fallen head over heels in love with him."

"Peter is rather handsome."

"Yeah," Sally said and bit her tongue from saying anything more. He was ex-actly the kind of handsome that flipped her stomach and made her toes tingle. "But I don't want to be interested in him, because Norma Jean is."

"Is Peter interested in her?"

"He doesn't seem to be. He said he wasn't. And he acted like he wanted to pursue a relationship with me. And his brother told me about the accountant position that was open on his farm. So I kinda thought that maybe his brother wanted us to get together too. Or he just knew I needed a job."

"It is hard to tell with men. Usually, they are kinda clueless about setting people up, but I've certainly known guys who could get into that kind of thing."

"Well, anyway, Norma Jean keeps push-ing between Peter and me, and..."

"You pushed back?" Lana guessed.

"No. I gave up. I gave in and gave her what she wanted. She wanted to dance with Peter at the Beach Bash, and I walked away from her, even though I wanted to dance with him. And when I went to Peter's office to volunteer for the job, as Peter was hiring me, Norma Jean came in and demanded the job. And I gave it to her."

"You gave it to her? Wasn't it Peter's to give?"

"I told him that I didn't want it anymore, and she could have it."

"I see."

"I know it seems kind of weird, but Norma Jean and I have been friends since kindergarten."

"She's not always very nice to you."

"No. But I don't want her friendship and the way she treats me to influence the way I treat her. I mean, isn't that what Jesus said? That we're supposed to be kind to everyone? We're not supposed to worry about how they treat us. And I can put some buts in there, but Jesus didn't give us any buts. He said we were supposed to be kind, even to people who are unkind to us."

"Love your enemies, bless them that curse you, do good to them that hate you, and pray for them which despitefully use you, and persecute you; That ye may be the children of your Father which is in heaven."

"Exactly. I don't think that Norma Jean is my enemy exactly, but isn't this me living what Jesus said?"

"You know, maybe I can learn a few things from you. Because before you pointed out that verse, I was going to recommend that you stand up for your rights and don't let Norma Jean push you around. But if you're going to live that verse, you're absolutely right. You give and keep giving, even if people are, what the world would say, taking advantage of you. You've never heard Jesus in any of his teachings say don't let anyone take advantage of you. Here, he's basically saying do let people take advantage of you. Isn't it crazy how that goes against what so many Christian teachers teach?"

"Maybe that's what's making me doubt everything. Or maybe it's because Peter's a really great guy, and I kind of feel like maybe... I don't know, I wouldn't mind ending up with someone like that, you know?"

"He would be a wonderful person to end up with. I have not heard anything but good things about him. He's a hard worker, honest, and he loves Jesus. There's really nothing else he needs."

"Yeah. That's exactly what I was thinking and why I was kind of castigating myself for not fighting a little harder for him or at least for the job anyway, you know?"

"I think you did the right thing. I know that that's probably not the advice that anyone else in the world would give you, but I think that being kind to people who are not kind to you and giving up your way for someone else, for what they want, is clearly what Jesus teaches."

"Sometimes Jesus's teachings are hard. I wish I could just do what I want, rather than feeling guilty for not doing what he says."

"You know, doing what he wants always leads to something better. Something better than what we think that we would get if we were doing things our own way."

"I guess it takes a lot of faith to believe that sometimes, especially when you're sitting where I'm sitting right now, out here along the lake by myself instead of in the office with Peter."

"Norma Jean might not be in the office with Peter. He might be avoiding the office when she's in it."

Sally laughed, but it was a short laugh. She didn't really wish any ill will on Norma Jean. "Maybe they're meant to be together, and now that I'm out of the picture, he's figured out that he actually really does love her."

"Or he's getting even more annoyed with her the more time he spends with her."

"You really know how to make a person feel better. I appreciate that."

"Oh, you know, a girl can dream."

"Really?" Sally looked over at Lana. "You've been single for a while. Are you dreaming about someone in particular?"

And as Sally watched, she was surprised to see that Lana's cheeks reddened and she gave a self-deprecating smile.

"I think I'm too old to have schoolgirl dreams."

"But I'm not too old to have schoolgirl dreams?"

"Yeah. I didn't mean to insult you. I meant... When you get to be my age, there's too much water under the bridge to start fresh with someone, you know? You'll have history, scars, baggage, and I know I'm more than a little set in my ways. I just can't imagine...things working out between me and someone else. Plus, I will be a lot more picky than I used to be."

"I don't see how I can get any pickier."

"Being picky is okay. But looking for perfection is not. After all, if you're looking for the perfect guy, he's going to be disappointed in you, since you are not perfect."

"That's a good point." Sally laughed again. "I wasn't really looking for a perfect guy. I just want someone who's not going to cheat on me, you know? Is it terrible to have standards that are that low?"

"You want character. That's what that is. Plus, you want someone who's going to work hard too. The Bible clearly teaches that the man is supposed to be taking care of the woman. Not the other way around."

"We don't listen to much of what the Bible says anymore."

"I think we'd be happier if we did. Although, I think happiness is a choice as well, and that's not always a popular idea."

"I agree with you there. Maybe it would be easier to choose happiness if we were doing what God wanted us to do, instead of what the world tells us to."

"Yeah. There'd be a lot less broken families anyway."

Lana's words were sad, and they made Sally feel bad. Lana's family was one of those broken families, where the husband hadn't stayed around, hadn't done what God taught, and instead chased after his own way.

Sally figured that was probably something that a woman never got over, even though Lana seemed to be happy and joyful and kind and motherly. There were still scars, like she had just said.

"What should I do? Just let it all go?"

"Has Peter tried to contact you again?"

"No. He hasn't." Sally couldn't keep the disappointment out of her voice.

"Well, I suppose, if we don't want to take Norma Jean from Peter, maybe we can get her to fall in love with someone?"

Sally's breath caught in her throat. That was a brilliant idea.

"But who?" she asked, going through her mind, thinking of all the men who might be available. Norma Jean really was a great person. She wasn't always the nicest person, but she really did work hard, and she did try to do right; she just wasn't always successful, not that Sally was. She could hardly fault Norma Jean.

"I don't know," Lana said after a little while as she gazed at the lake, watching the waves crash on the shore and a pair of eagles fly overhead.

"And there won't be anyone new in town until next spring or summer."

"Don't be so sure about that. You know, sometimes the Lord works in mysterious ways. That doesn't mean that we can't help things along a little," Lana said with a chuckle in her voice. After all, that's exactly what they were just doing.

Helping the Lord along by trying to figure out someone else for Norma Jean to fall in love with.

"I tried the matchmaking thing once, and it ended up backfiring."

"If you're talking about accidentally locking Eleanor and Franklin in the shack together, I clearly think that worked out perfectly. After all, they're married and very happily by the looks of things. I think you did a pretty excellent job there if I do say so myself."

Sally laughed. She hadn't come any closer to figuring anything out except she was probably right about giving up what she wanted for her friend. That made her feel a little better, and she wasn't quite as despondent as she'd been. After all, God promised to reward those who obeyed Him, and she had certainly obeyed Him by giving more than was required.

"All right, I suppose I'd better head on down the beach. I promised someone I would go see them today, and I want to keep my word. If I think of anyone who would be good for Norma Jean, I'll let you know."

"Thanks. Do you want me to walk with you?" Sally asked.

"You can if you want to, but I'm fine, I do this four or five times a week. It's good exercise for me, just getting out and feeling the wind on my face and seeing the lake and the sky and just all of God's creation. It gives me a good reset in my head."

"Yeah. I guess that's what I'm doing right now."

Lana waved and walked off, and she turned her face back toward the lake.

Whether she should try to manipulate the situation and find someone else for Norma Jean, or whether she should just look for another job and let it all go, trusting God to work things out, she wasn't sure. Actually, when she put it like that, it was obvious that she should just trust God to work things out.

Although, maybe He was going to work things out by finding someone else for Norma Jean to fall in love with, and He wanted her to help Him with that.

She laughed at herself and the way she would do almost anything to make what she thought God wanted line up with what she wanted.

Chapter 8

Norma Jean strode from the desk to the window and then moved to another window. She did that the whole way around the room, until she came back to the window she started with.

Nothing. There was no one outside in any direction that she could see. Just fenced pasture with big ugly cows in them.

Peter was nowhere around. He hadn't been around much since the first day he hired her, and she'd been working eight hours a day, five days a week for two weeks now.

It's Friday, and he left her paycheck on her desk. It was there when she walked in that morning.

She had thought that she'd at least see him when he handed it to her. That's why she checked the box that she wanted a paper check rather than direct deposit.

But it felt like he'd outsmarted her.

She could make up a question to ask, text him, and get him to come. She'd done that multiple times over the last two weeks. But it got to the point where he had said to just write down all of her questions and he'd come in fifteen minutes before she was ready to leave and answer them all.

She felt like he was doing it right before she left so that she wouldn't be tempted to drag the question-and-answer sessions out. And he wouldn't have to spend any more time than necessary with her.

Pursing her lips and narrowing her eyes, she looked out at the field. She actually asked Peter three times now if he needed any help on the farm besides what she was doing as his accountant.

Every time, he brushed her off. But she wanted to work with the animals. Actually, no. She wanted to work with Peter. How was she supposed to get Peter to like her if he refused to spend any time with her?

She pursed her lips again and looked back at the desk. She could make up another problem, or...she could go open that gate and let the cows out. She wouldn't have to tell anyone that she let the cows out herself, and when Peter came, she could run out and help him. That way, they'd be spending some time together, and maybe he'd see that she wasn't afraid of the cows, and he'd let her help him on the farm.

She almost rubbed her hands together in anticipation as she grabbed her puffer vest and beanie hat and threw them on quickly before she hurried outside.

It didn't take any time at all to open the gate, but then she stood there for a moment, wondering how she was going to get the cows to see that the gate was open and they could go ahead and walk out.

But she couldn't stand by the gate long, because she didn't want anyone to know that she was the one who opened it.

On that thought, she practically ran back to the little building that housed the office and hurried back inside.

She wanted to stand by the window and watch to see when the cows got out, but she would be better able to pretend surprise if she actually was surprised when someone showed up. So, she took her hat and vest off and went back over and sat down at the desk.

She got immersed in spreadsheets, in balancing everything and checking the receipts off. She truly did love that kind of work, and time just flew by as she worked the numbers.

So, it really did surprise her when she heard a shout outside. It took her a few minutes to come back to reality before she remembered what was going on and jumped up.

She looked out the window first and saw Peter's hired guy, she thought his name was Miles. He'd been in the office several times, twice to get his paycheck and once to turn in a few receipts. He was nice, handsome in a ruggedly cowboy type way.

Of course, he wasn't the boss, and that was who she wanted.

Still, he was rounding up some cattle and shouted something to Peter, who worked further over across the driveway as she watched.

She couldn't hear what he said, but her eyes were drawn to Peter, and immediately her heart stopped and her hand went to her throat.

A cow, one that was bigger than all the rest of them—could it be a bull?—was running straight toward Peter

"Oh no. What have I done?" she said to herself as she ran outside, completely forgetting about her hat and vest.

She stopped on the porch. She didn't want to get hurt, and that animal was big. With its head lowered, it looked mean too.

Peter, looking up at Miles to see what he was yelling about, didn't have time to turn around and see what Miles gestured toward.

The animal hit him before he had a chance to even try to get away, and the impact made him fly through the air, crashing into a heap on the ground.

Norma Jean's legs wanted to take her there, but fear held her to the porch, because the large animal was not yet contained. She put her fist in her mouth as her horrified eyes seemed to be frozen on Peter, who had not moved from the spot where he lay on the ground. The bull, at least that's what Norma Jean had decided it must be, seemed to lose sight of him for a moment before it lowered its head and charged at the still form.

This time, a sound escaped from Norma Jean's mouth as she realized Peter's leg had been crumpled at an unnatural angle. She saw that, just before the bull drove his head into Peter's side.

She'd forgotten about Miles, but he sprinted from the other side of the driveway to the unfenced field where the bull was with Peter.

At his side was a small dog, which made Norma Jean want to run forward just to grab the dog and get it out of its way, but to her surprise, the dog darted toward the bull, getting in front of him and grabbing onto his nose.

The bull shook his head and lifted the dog off its feet. But the dog was able to get the bull to move backward, away from Peter's body.

That's when Norma Jean realized she should call the ambulance.

Running inside, grabbing her phone off the corner of the desk where she set it earlier, she dialed 911 as she ran back outside.

By that time, the bull had slammed the dog to the ground, but as Norma Jean watched, the dog popped right back up and ran at the bull again. This time, it came in from behind and kept the bull moving forward and to the side.

The bull had apparently forgotten about Peter, so the dog had done a good job of distracting it, and then as Miles shouted a few commands, the dog herded the bull back into the pasture.

Miles had the dog take the bull clear to the middle of the pasture, rounding up several cows along with him, which was probably a smart idea since when Miles pulled the dog off, the bull stayed with the cows and the dog ran back.

Miles was already over beside Peter, kneeling down.

"I called an ambulance," Norma Jean said breathlessly as she reached his side.

"Yeah. Good." Miles didn't say anything else, but he lifted his head, looked around, and gave a few more commands to the dog, who then rounded up the rest of the cows and took them back into the pasture field.

Meanwhile, Miles put several fingers on Peter's neck. "There's a pulse."

"Thank God," Norma Jean said fervently.

"I don't want to move him, just in case he has some kind of back injury," Miles said, and Norma Jean thought that was a good idea.

"I didn't stay on long enough to ask how long it would be till they got here. I told him I had to go, because I wasn't sure if there was something I needed to do or could help with."

"Whoever left the gate open has done enough," Miles said, and Norma Jean felt fear pulling tight in her stomach. She was the one who left the gate open.

But she hadn't meant for anyone to get hurt. Would people believe her?

"I'm so glad you're here. And your dog. That was amazing," she said, kneeling down beside Peter and taking one of his hands, flinching because the position in which Peter lay looked so uncomfortable.

"A good dog is better than ten men," Miles said, without taking his eyes off Peter.

His voice was deep and rough, and it somehow made Norma Jean feel a little better, even though he wasn't trying to reassure her about anything.

"Do you think Peter's going to die?" she said, feeling so guilty she could hardly stand it.

"No. I don't. I didn't see anything that caused me to think that he had a fatal injury. But he'll have a big headache when he wakes up, and it looks to me like his leg is broken." Miles sighed. "There might be some ribs as well, but I don't know." His voice trailed off, like he was trying to make Peter's injuries sound like they weren't quite as bad as what they were, in order for Norma Jean to not worry.

She appreciated that about him, but at the moment, all she could think of was how guilty she felt, and how she wished she could go back and do the last thirty minutes all over again.

No, she'd go back further. After all, she was selfish and mean, and sometimes she knew it, but she just didn't care because it got her what she wanted.

She had never meant to hurt anyone. Not at all.

"When the ambulance comes, you're going to have to ride with him, because I'm going to need to stay here. We have a load of calves in the trailer, and I can't just let them sit there."

"I have to be in the office because there's at least four different people who are coming in to pick up a check today. Plus, I have cash for someone else who was supposed to stop in so Peter could pay for the minerals he got."

Miles was already taking his phone out of his pocket. "I should have called his brother to begin with."

He pushed a few buttons, held the phone to his ear, but pulled it back down without saying anything.

"It went straight to voicemail." He sighed. "I hate to send him to the hospital by himself, but neither one of us can go." His voice trailed off as a siren wailed in the distance.

"Thank you, Jesus," Norma Jean said. She had been afraid that Peter would die before the ambulance could even get to him. She wanted to go to the hospital with him, but it was probably more important that she handle things that he couldn't now. Especially since this was all her fault.

"Sally would go," Norma Jean said before she really thought about it. She suspected that Sally liked Peter as much as Peter seemed to like Sally. Norma Jean had been sure that if she had been able to spend time with Peter, Peter would forget all about Sally and focus on her, but right now, she just wanted things to go well for Peter and to do the very best she could for him, and she couldn't leave her job. He had people who were depending on him for their money, and she couldn't let him down.

"Sounds like the ambulance is going to be here before she could get here. You can tell her to just meet him at the hospital."

"Yeah. Maybe we can tell the first responders that she'll be there."

"They probably won't let anyone but family in, not unless he asks for her."

Norma Jean nodded. She wasn't very familiar with the etiquette for emergency room visits, but she trusted what Miles said to be true.

"I'll call her," she said, dialing Sally's number with trembling fingers.

"Hello?" Sally answered after two rings.

"Sally. I need a big favor."

"Sure. Anything," Sally said easily, and that was part of what Norma Jean loved about her. Sally would do anything for anyone if she possibly could.

"Peter's been hurt."

Sally gasped. "Peter? Hurt?"

"Yeah. He was...charged by a bull."

"Oh my goodness. Is he...okay?"

"He still breathing, and Miles said he still had a heartbeat. But I was hoping that you could meet him at the hospital. Miles can't go, and I'm supposed to be meeting people for checks and to give them cash, and I hate to leave without doing what Peter told me to do. Especially since he's not going to be here to do it."

"Of course. I'm leaving right away. What hospital?"

"I assume the Blueberry Beach hospital, but I'll let you know if the first responders say different. They're pulling in now," Norma Jean said as she lifted her head and watched the ambulance with flashing lights pull into the driveway.

"All right. I'll be there."

"I'll give one of the first responders your telephone number so they can text you and let you know what's going on."

"Great idea. Thanks."

The ambulance pulled in as Norma Jean swiped off. Her hands were still trembling, and her heart beat faster than she ever felt it beat before. This was all her fault, and she felt awful. She was so thankful that Miles was there to handle everything, because she would have been a mess. What a stupid thing to do. But the fact that she wouldn't do it again didn't change the fact that she shouldn't have done it to begin with.

It took the first responders a long time to get Peter straightened out and onto a board where they secured his head so that he wouldn't move around in case he had a spinal injury.

By the time he left, Norma Jean was freezing cold, but she didn't want to go inside. Peter had to be cold too, but he hadn't woken up the whole time. Which worried her.

"This is terrible," she said, looking down at the ground as the taillights slowly moved away.

Miles stared at the back of the ambulance. "Yeah. If there was ever a nicer guy, I've never met him. Peter is one of a kind."

"I know," Norma Jean said softly.

"You did a good job. You look cold. You probably ought to go inside." His heavy hand came down on her shoulder, and while it was rough, it felt comforting, exactly as his voice did.

Without thinking, she reached up and touched his fingers.

"I'm scared," she said softly. She couldn't explain any more. He wouldn't understand that she wasn't scared for Peter, she was scared for herself.

Well, she was scared for Peter, but she wasn't just scared for Peter.

"I think Peter will be fine. Blueberry Beach has some of the best doctors in the state. Doctors move here to get out of Chicago, and they bring their years of expertise with them. He will be in good hands."

She swallowed and looked up into Miles's face. If it had been another time, different circumstances, a different situation, she might have...blinked her eyes coyly at him and tried to flirt. He was...strong and capable and very manly, a man's man, which was the total opposite of her, and she loved those differences.

Instead, he squeezed her shoulder, dropped his hand, and said, "Do you need me to walk you to the door?"

Maybe it was because she hadn't moved, but she thought it was very gentleman-ly of him to ask. She shook her head. She was not going to think about anyone else. She didn't deserve to have some-one when she treated the person that she was infatuated with so terribly.

Peter was lying on a hospital bed, in an ambulance, and who knew if he would ever walk again, let alone survive. She couldn't just flip affections from Peter to Miles at the drop of a hat. She would be completely devoted to Peter for the rest of her life.

With that thought, she shook her head and said, "No, thank you." And then, with renewed purpose, she turned on her toes and marched into the office building. She would sit in that office chair and she would work until she dropped if it would benefit Peter.

Chapter 9

"He's awake and asking for you," Franklin said as he opened the door to the waiting room.

Sally jerked her head up, relief flooding through her. "For me?"

Franklin nodded. "He asked about you almost immediately."

Sally wanted to smile over that, but she wanted to make sure that Peter wasn't about to die, first. "What did the doctor say?"

"Peter can tell you all the details, but basically, he's got a hard head and he's gonna live." Franklin stifled a yawn. "I'm going to head home. I already said good-bye to him. He's going to call me if any-thing changes, but it's been a long day."

Sally nodded.

"Visiting hours are over, but the nurses said you could go back. Call me if you need anything?"

"I will," Sally said. She was glad the nurs-es were allowing her to go back. She'd been sitting there for four hours, and she was gratified that Peter had been asking about her, although she hadn't expected that. But she didn't dwell on it, because her whole focus was on seeing Peter and finding out how he was doing.

Franklin led her back to Peter's room, waved at Peter lying in the bed, and then nodded at Sally before he turned and strode down the hall.

Sally tiptoed into the room.

"You can walk closer," Peter said, grinning a bit from the bed. Then he winced. Like his smiling had brought on some pain.

"Are you okay?"

"Feels like I've gotten run over by a one-ton bull. Oh wait, I did."

Sally tried not to giggle. Maybe it was a combination of nerves, but also Peter was funny. She knew that, and it was one of the things that drew her. She liked anyone who could make her smile, and Peter always could.

"I hear it on good authority that the bull is just fine," Sally said.

"I know I'm supposed to say that's good to know, but I'm not feeling it right now."

Sally grinned again, but her smile faded as he winced.

"Every time I smile, it makes the headache pound a little sharper." He closed his eyes. "But I'm glad you came back."

"Of course. Norma Jean said that she had things to do in the office and that Miles had animals to take care of, and I said I would stay with you. Of course, the hospital personnel wouldn't let me come back, even though I asked several times."

"You could have told them you were my mother."

Sally put her hands on her hips and pretended to be offended. "I'm going to turn around and walk right back out of this hospital room if you don't take that back right now."

"I could have said you could have pretended to be my wife. Would that have upset you just as much?"

"I'll pretend to be your daughter. How's that?"

It was his turn to snort and wince.

"I'm sorry," she said immediately.

"No. It's okay. I'd rather be wincing from the pain of a smile than not having any reason to laugh."

"I guess that's one way to look at it. But I think the doctors would say that we should keep things quiet and just let you rest."

"That's exactly what the doctor would say," a nurse said as she walked in with her iPad clipped to one arm while she typed a couple of things in it, then held her lanyard against it until it beeped.

"I just have to check a few things out here. Give me a minute, and then I'll be out of your hair," the nurse said cheerfully.

"She told me last time she was in that I would live. It was a relief." Peter spoke with his eyes closed.

"I'll say. I was pretty relieved when I heard that you were expected to make it. But they did say you broke one of the bones in your leg."

"Actually, both of the bones in my lower leg."

"I guess when he decides to break a leg, he does a bang-up job," the nurse said as she checked the fluid level and then typed something else into her iPad.

After punching a few buttons on the monitor beside his bed, taking his blood pressure and temperature, she hurried back out of the room.

Sally had made her way over to the far side of the bed and sat down on the edge of the chair. "I guess I should have asked her how long I'm allowed to stay."

"Stay until they kick you out. At least, I'd appreciate it if you did."

"Happily. I... I was terrified when they said that you were in a crumpled heap on the ground and weren't moving."

"Yeah. I should have known better. I knew there was a bull in that pasture, but I was hoping to get the cows rounded up before they spread all through that field. Once we lose them, they're often hard to find, and I didn't want them to trample the neighbor's winter wheat."

"Were you able to get them all?"

"I don't know. I... I got taken out of the game, I guess."

"I see. I could call Norma Jean—"

"No!" The volume of his voice didn't change, but the emphatic way he said "no" made Sally freeze as her hand started to move toward her phone. "Please don't bring her into this."

"I'm sorry," Sally said, putting her hand back in her lap.

"You know, for the last two weeks I've answered about a hundred ridiculously stupid questions every day. And normally, I don't really mind answering people's questions. If you don't know, you don't know. But if you're just making up stuff that you don't know, it's annoying." He cracked an eye. "Do you mind telling me why you backed off and gave Norma Jean the job?"

"Well, technically, you gave her the job, since it wasn't mine to give."

"I wanted to give it to you."

"I'm sorry. I…" She sighed. She didn't normally go around talking about Norma Jean's past, but it wasn't exactly a secret in the town they grew up in, just…that wasn't Strawberry Sands and most people didn't know the things that had happened to her.

"Norma Jean had a rough life. I mean, we've been friends since kindergarten, and my mom wouldn't let me go over to her house because it was too dangerous. Her mom was an alcoholic, she had boyfriends in and out. She couldn't keep a job, maybe because of the alcohol or maybe because of the on-again, off-again drug habit she had. Regardless, Norma Jean spent a lot of time at my house."

"I didn't know."

"Most people don't. And it's something I don't tell everyone. I just... Maybe she's jealous of me. Everyone has struggles, but I had so much that she didn't. I... I probably should have done a little better in my life than what I have, considering how great my start was."

"You haven't done poorly."

"I guess not. But Norma Jean is a true success story. She really did come from nothing."

"Sounds to me like your family helped her a good bit."

"We did. But all the help in the world doesn't mean anything if you don't take advantage of it. I think Norma Jean got to the point where she felt like she had to take advantage of everything."

"Including you."

"You know, Lana and I were just talking about that not long ago. That there isn't any place in the Bible where it says that you shouldn't allow people to take advantage of you. In fact, Jesus almost commands us to allow people to take advantage of us. But yet, in our society today, even Christians say we shouldn't allow it."

"I guess you're right. I know what verse you're talking about, and I have to agree with you. Jesus does say bless those who persecute you. Bless and not curse. We are also commanded to be kind to everyone. Everyone. Not just people who are kind and considerate to us."

"Yes. That's the one. And there's nothing in Scripture that tells us that there is a limit on that. In fact, when Jesus talks about forgiving people, he says seventy times seven. He's just basically saying that it should be an awful lot of forgiveness."

"Well, I think you qualify for sainthood in that area."

"I don't. Because sometimes I get irritated."

"And rightfully so."

"No. I don't want to. I want to be willing to give whatever people need from me without resenting it. You know?"

"That's too good to be true. And it's probably not good for you."

"If we're talking about our emotional health in regards to what a psychiatrist might say, then you're right. But if we're talking about spiritual health and what God might say, then I have to respectfully disagree."

He was quiet for a bit, then shook his head slowly, with his face tightening up as he did so as though the motion irritated his headache. "I can't argue with that."

"Thank you. Norma Jean is...difficult. You know that, but she's also someone God loves. And God somehow chose me to be in her life. To be a person who loves her unconditionally. And yes, I know, when you give someone too much, you tend to spoil them. They don't have to grow their character, but you do realize that when you're giving, their character might not be growing, but your character is."

"I never thought about it that way."

"It's true. I mean, I'm definitely not for spoiling children. A parent's job is to teach them to have character, so a lot of times, you have to do things that they don't like. But in friendship and relationships, why wouldn't you be the one to give more? I know when you do it, it seems like the other person is quote, unquote, winning, but in reality, it's you that's actually becoming a better person because you've learned to give up your way, give up your 'rights,' and to be kind to someone even when it's hard. That type of character is forged in the fire of hardship, whether it's hardship in giving up your rights or hardship in some other kind of sacrifice."

"That's an interesting way to look at it."

"I believe it's a biblical way."

"I don't want it to be. I want you to want to be with me more than you want to be nice to Norma Jean."

She laughed a little, because that made her feel good. That Peter really did want her. "Well, there also is that friendship rule where if your friend has her eye on someone, you can't step in between them. That to me is a loyalty thing."

"And I admire your loyalty. That's one of the things I really like about you, but I want you to be loyal to me."

"Well, I really can't pursue that, not until Norma Jean decides that she doesn't want you anymore. I mean, isn't that the way it goes?"

"I don't know. I suppose. If my brother had his eye on a girl, I definitely wouldn't step in between them, even if I really liked her. But while I understand it, it feels like if I say no to her, all bets are off."

"It should, but I'm pretty sure Norma Jean wouldn't see it that way."

They didn't say anything for a while, and she thought that maybe he had fallen asleep. He seemed a little loopy from the pain meds; although this conversation was certainly lucid, he'd probably said things he normally wouldn't. He almost certainly wouldn't be admitting that he had feelings for her, wanted to spend more time with her, if he wasn't under the influence of whatever drugs they had given him.

"I wish there was a way we could get Norma Jean to set her sights on someone else."

"I wish there was too," she agreed softly.

They didn't say anything for a while, and Sally ran through the ideas in her head. It was kind of funny that Peter had said the same thing that Lana had said earlier. Still, there was no solution in sight.

Peter shifted a little, and immediately Sally straightened.

"Are you okay?"

"Are you going to ask that every time I move?" he said, one side of his mouth working up.

"If I have to. I mean, are you hurting?"

"A little. As long as I have it settled just so, it only throbs. The doc said eight weeks in a cast, and I can handle that."

"It'll probably make for restless sleep."

"Maybe. They've got some pretty good drugs in here though. I might be okay."

"They've loosened your tongue a bit, I think," she teased.

"No. I don't think I said anything to you tonight that I didn't want to say. I just... Maybe the drugs gave me a little bit of bravery that I should have had anyway."

She didn't answer that, because she wasn't sure how.

"The X-ray showed that my ribs were clear. But they were bruised. I can feel them, and it hurts to take a deep breath. It also hurts to laugh, but I'm not going to quit laughing just because of a little pain."

"What about your head?"

"Concussion for sure, but I think they're going to tell me to just take it easy, which I have to do anyway because of the broken leg."

"I see."

He opened an eye. "The doctor asked me if I had anyone at home to take care of me. I told him I lived by myself... But I thought I could hire a nurse." He smiled, and Sally had to return his grin.

"I do have some nursing experience."

"I know."

"But..."

"Norma Jean."

Sally nodded.

"You know, I talked to Miles some. He's quiet, although he's a good man. He's good with animals, and he has his dog, Chester, trained really well. From the little bit I talked to him, Chester was able to get the bull's attention off me. He told me I owed Chester my life."

"Seems like if Miles was the one who trained the dog, Miles deserves a little bit of gratitude."

"That's what I said. But at the time, I wasn't really up to talking a whole lot."

"I feel like you need to rest now."

"If I rest, are you going to stay?" He turned his head to the side and looked at her. "That's not fair. It's late. You need to go home and get some rest."

"No. I'll stay. I... I want to." It was true. She did. She didn't really know why though. There wasn't anything for her to do. And she wasn't his mom, like he had suggested, and she wasn't his daughter either. She...wasn't anything to him. She didn't really have the right to stay. Plus, what she said about Norma Jean was true. She wasn't going to pursue Peter, or allow there to be anything there, until Norma Jean had decided she didn't want him.

With another person, that wouldn't take long with Peter not showing any interest, but with Norma Jean, it was quite possible that she would spend the next five years trying to catch Peter's eye. Norma Jean could be like a dog with a bone once she had her eye on something.

She had risen from her difficult beginnings and become a successful and almost normal adult by having grit and determination and perseverance.

Really, Norma Jean had a lot of great characteristics. She was just human like everyone else and had flaws. Sometimes those flaws were hard to swallow, but they weren't any worse or any better than anybody else's flaws.

The hospital chair wasn't super comfortable, but once Peter's breathing had evened out and Sally was sure he was asleep, she settled down more comfortably and put her hand on Peter's. She didn't thread their fingers together, but she held onto it, sliding the chair so she could lay her head on the back and still hold his hand.

It was late when she finally fell asleep, wondering how they could work this whole situation out.

Chapter 10

Peter woke slowly, groggy, and didn't remember at first why his head pounded and his leg sent sharp pain up his hip and out both elbows.

As he tried to turn, his ribs yanked sharp pain back down, as though answering his leg.

He would rather not have his body parts fighting with each other, but it helped a little bit to swim out of the groggy, drug-induced sleep, and he was able to remember that he'd been run over by a bull, and he couldn't expect to not feel pain from that.

He was going to be laid up for a while. That was frustrating.

But it might be a lot less frustrating if Sally could be convinced to be his nurse.

Except, the problem was, even if he could convince Sally to do it—she seemed receptive to the idea last night if he remembered correctly—there was still Norma Jean between them. And he hadn't quite figured out what he was going to do about that.

Norma Jean was loud, brash, bold. She wasn't afraid to go after what she wanted, and while he appreciated Sally telling him about her life and her childhood, and he could appreciate the fact that she needed to become that way in order to be successful, it didn't make it any easier for him to try to figure out how to handle her.

He didn't want to hurt her, especially now that he understood where Sally was coming from. He appreciated the fact that she was so sweet and gracious with someone that most people would have been completely annoyed with and ditched long ago. Maybe that would have made Norma Jean grow up, but it was like Sally said, every time a person gave in to someone else, they were growing their own character. Which is why Sally had really matured spiritually, while Norma Jean had been stunted.

As he lay there thinking about that, he slowly realized that Sally was still curled up in the chair, which made him smile, but his heart did a loop when he also realized she sat in such a way that she could reach to hold his hand. She had her hand hooked around his, and he hadn't even realized that he squeezed her fingers, not in a death grip exactly, but nice and tight. Like he didn't want to let go. Which was exactly right. He didn't want to let go.

She looked just as beautiful to him in slumber as she did when she was awake, and he took a few minutes to just admire her.

She probably wouldn't like the way she looked. In his experience, women typically didn't. But he wasn't used to waking up with one either.

Still, her hair was messy, her cheek all bunched up where it rested against the edge of the chair, and unless he was mistaken, there was a little bit of drool coming out of the corner of her mouth.

But she was beautiful to him.

The way she treated Norma Jean, the way she allowed herself to be put aside, the way she didn't get angry but thought of the other person first. He didn't really know anyone else like that and appreciated the fact that Sally hadn't tried to pull any punches with him. She hadn't beat around the bush, and she'd been right in her assessment of the Bible.

She was putting into practice a verse that he knew but conveniently did not recognize in the situation they were in. Funny how a person could know what the Bible said but either forget it or rationalize it away.

As he watched, she stirred a little, and he waited, wondering how she would react when she realized where she was and what she was doing.

He didn't loosen the grip on her hand at all, because he really didn't want her to pull her fingers away. Of course, if she tugged, he'd let go.

But he didn't want to.

Chapter 11

Norma Jean didn't feel any better the next day when she arrived two hours early for work.

Perhaps her early arrival time had something to do with the fact that she knew that Peter was in the hospital right now because of her.

She hadn't been able to sleep at all and knew she looked terrible this morning. Hopefully no one showed up at the office and wanted anything.

She had barely gotten that thought out of her head as she stood at her desk, tapping her fingers on it and trying to decide what to do, when there was a sound at the door before a little girl ran into the room, followed by Miles.

"Hey! You're pretty. What's your name?" the little girl said before Norma Jean could recover from the shock.

Miles did not look like the type of guy who would have a cute little girl with two little pigtails bouncing behind her running around beside him.

"I'm Norma Jean."

"You can call her Miss Norma Jean," Miles said immediately after she spoke her name.

The little girl looked at her daddy, gave him an angelic grin, batted her big brown eyes at him, and then looked back at Norma Jean. "Miss Norma Jean, my name's Holly." Holly continued over to her, her little hand held out, her other hand behind her back like she was going to the showcase showdown.

Norma Jean hardly thought Holly was old enough to know what a showcase showdown was, and in fact, Norma Jean figured that probably wasn't something anyone of her generation should know either. But she'd spent enough time with Sally watching TV while she was caring for her Aunt Wilma that the showcase showdown was pretty much etched into her brain.

Regardless, she took the little hand, bent over a bit, and shook very seriously.

"Very nice to meet you, Miss Holly." Norma Jean's heart melted at the little girl's sweet expression contrasted with the serious way she shook her hand. "I haven't seen you around before."

"I'm here sometimes."

Miles explained, "Normally when my ex doesn't show up to get Holly, I don't come in to work. But considering what happened yesterday, I knew I couldn't do that today."

"Oh my goodness. I'm so glad you came. I have no idea what to do," Norma Jean said with her hand at her chest.

Miles didn't even crack a smile. That made Norma Jean all the more determined to get him to give her one.

"I'm going to have to ask you to watch her. She can't go out with me."

"But I want to, Daddy. I'm a big girl, remember? I'm your best worker. I can do it!" Holly skipped back over to her dad and looked pleadingly up into his unsmiling face.

"You are, sweetie." He patted her hair, but then he flattened his lips and shook his head. "But I can't have you around the dangerous equipment that I need to be using in order to feed the cows here. Back home, it's a little different."

"Please?"

Miles didn't say anything, he just raised his brows, and the little girl closed her mouth and her head dropped.

Norma Jean knew exactly how the little girl felt. She'd been told no so many times in her life, she started to think that was the only answer she would ever get. She couldn't really remember her parents ever saying yes to anything.

"If you want to, you can help me," she said, walking toward the little girl and then kneeling down in front of her.

"You mean it?" the little girl said, looking at Norma Jean from underneath her lashes.

"Really. I have so much work to do here, I don't even know where to start. I haven't even had coffee yet!"

"I can't make coffee." The little girl's head hung down. Then her face brightened. "But I can make hot chocolate! Daddy says I make the best hot chocolate any-where."

"My goodness. It just so happens that we have hot chocolate right here, and you can be in charge of making it. That's such a relief. Now I'll be able to get so many other things done if you are in charge of the hot chocolate this morning."

"Yay! I have a job!"

"I see that, honey," Miles said, his expression inscrutable, as he looked at Norma Jean from underneath his ball cap.

"I bet your daddy will be ready for a hot chocolate when he comes back from feeding the cows. It's cold outside this morning."

"I'll make the best hot chocolate ever," Holly said in her peppy little girl voice.

"I'll be expecting it when I get back. It will be an hour or so, maybe two if we have more cows out," he said, and he gave Norma Jean another look that made her knees want to knock together. It was like he knew she was the one who had left the gate open.

"Oh, I hope not. And if they are, you'll be careful, won't you?"

"Daddy has Chester. If there are any problems, Chester will take care of them. He's a great dog," Holly said helpfully.

"He looked like a good dog. I saw him working yesterday, and I was really impressed. Someone has spent a lot of time training him."

"Daddy did," Holly said, crossing her arms over her chest. "Daddy and me go out in the yard every night, and we go through Chester's commands. Sometimes Chester doesn't want to listen, but Daddy never gets mad. He says that it's important that Chester knows what you want. Because he wants to please him. He just has to understand."

Norma Jean lifted her eyebrows a little at that big lecture, and she peeked out of the corner of her eyes at Miles who seemed to be trying not to smile, if the quivering of his lips was any indication.

Normally Norma Jean might get a little bit jealous that this little whippersnapper of a kid could make Miles smile and she couldn't. But it seemed like she probably should want to be on the same side as Holly. Shouldn't she?

She had to think about that. But it would probably be better for her to warm up to Holly, and have Holly like her, than it would be to try to compete against her.

When she had been a kid, sometimes her mother's boyfriends had tried to use her to get to her mom, and then they tossed her aside. She didn't want to be that kind of person. She hadn't spent all the time climbing out of that pit just to jump back in as soon as she was around a little kid.

So, she had to do something different if she wanted things to change.

That little thread of jealousy had to go.

She tried to crush it out ruthlessly and figured that she needed to make sure that she watched her thoughts. That was where the jealousy started. She was going to love this little girl, whether Miles smiled at her or not. And that was that.

While she had been giving herself a lecture, Miles moved toward the door. "Are you sure you're okay?"

"I'm sure," Norma Jean said, looking at Miles just to make sure that he was actually talking to her and wasn't asking his daughter.

"All right then. I'll be back as soon as I can, but I'll want to make sure everything is done right. I'm guessing that it's going to be a little while before Peter is up to taking over again."

"Did you hear from him?" Norma Jean asked anxiously, thinking that she should have asked that to begin with.

"Yeah. Sorry." Miles rubbed the back of his neck. "I forgot to tell you. He's got a broken leg and a concussion, and they think his ribs are bruised, but they're not broken."

"Thank God. So... What does that mean?"

"I think they're going to be sending him home. They're putting his leg in a splint and perhaps casting it. He wasn't sure when I talked to him."

"So he might even be home today?" Norma Jean asked, remembering that she was supposed to be putting all her effort into being loyal to Peter. After all, she owed him. But Miles was such a huge distraction. She...felt a pull toward him that she had never felt before.

"He thought so. He wasn't going to know for sure until the orthopedic surgeon came in and talked to him."

"Surgeon?"

"He was pretty sure that the orthopedic surgeon was going to say he didn't need surgery, but until he heard it from the horse's mouth, so to speak, he wasn't going to say for sure."

"I see." She didn't know how any of that stuff worked, but an orthopedic surgeon sounded a little scary. Hopefully it was nothing.

"All right. I'm off." He put his hand on the doorknob, then turned around. "I'll give you my phone number in case you need me?"

It should have been a statement, but it ended up being a question as he looked at Norma Jean, then nodded his head at Holly who had wandered over to the coffee maker and stood with her hands behind her back. She bent over, looking at the different coffees that Norma Jean had arranged.

"Oh. Yeah. That would be a good idea," Norma Jean said, pulling her phone from where it sat on the desk and lifting it up while Miles told her his number.

She punched it and then sent him a text with a smiley face.

He didn't even wiggle an eyelash when he saw what she said.

She was going to have to up her game if she was going to get Miles to smile. And then she castigated herself. If she was interested in Peter, she couldn't be worried about whether or not Miles smiled at her.

"Thanks," he said, turning toward the door and then calling to his daughter, "Be good."

"See you later, Dad," Holly said as she ran toward him, throwing her arms around his neck and squeezing him tight as he bent down.

Norma Jean's heart felt happy as she watched the taciturn man put his arms around his daughter and hug her tightly. It was obvious he loved her and adored her and that she adored him.

Norma Jean didn't have any idea what happened between Miles and his wife. As far as she knew, Miles was from Raspberry Ridge, which was a little town farther north along the lake.

She busied herself at her desk so they didn't catch her staring, and he walked out without saying anything more.

Holly stood in front of the door, watching her dad walk away. "At home, when we feed, Daddy lets me help him."

"Wow. He must really love having such a great helper."

"Yeah. I'm his biggest helper," Holly said, turning around and giving Norma Jean a big smile.

"We don't have as many cows as what Mr. Peter does though. And Daddy has to come down here to work so he has enough money to feed me. I eat a lot," she said, and Norma Jean had to work to hide a big smile over Holly obviously repeating what she'd heard her dad say.

"I'm glad that he's able to help Mr. Peter, because Mr. Peter is going to need a lot of help if he's got a broken leg."

"Yeah. Dad said that if he could have gotten there a little bit earlier, Chester could have kept it all from happening, but Mr. Peter was in a big rush because he didn't want his cows to get into the neighbor's field."

"I see," Norma Jean said. She didn't believe in pumping little kids for information and definitely not because a person was interested in their father. However, for the child's own good and welfare, she said, "Does your mommy help on the farm?"

The little girl's face dropped. "No. Mommy moved to Chicago. She has a boyfriend there."

"Oh." Now Norma Jean had opened the can of worms, and she didn't know what to say. Obviously the idea of her mother having a boyfriend in Chicago and not living with them anymore made Holly sad.

"Mommy says I can come visit her some-time, but she hasn't let me come yet. She is supposed to come and play with me on Thursdays, but she didn't come today."

"Maybe she was just late."

"She said she'd come twice next week, but she says that all the time and then she never does."

"How old are you?" Norma Jean said, thinking that the little girl should be in school.

"I'm five." Norma Jean didn't have to ask the question, because Holly continued. "And I was supposed to go to kindergarten this year, but with all the stuff at our house, Daddy said that he would wait and send me next year. He said maybe if we did a little school this year, I could just go to first grade, and I wouldn't need kindergarten."

"I see. And have you been working on schoolwork?"

"A little bit. But Dad had a lot of work to do on the farm, and now he has to help Mr. Peter a whole lot more too, I'm not sure if he'll have time." The little girl shrugged her shoulders and then said, "Should I start the hot chocolate?"

"Well, if your dad is going to take an hour, we probably ought to start the hot chocolate five minutes before he's going to get here. Otherwise, it will be cold. But we can practice making hot chocolate, and you and I can taste it to make sure it's okay?"

Holly smiled real big. "Yeah. I don't think I need any practice, but you can taste my hot chocolate and see if it's good."

"All right. Let's do that." She walked over to the display she had out and chatted with Holly as she pointed out the hot chocolate and helped her with the hot water.

If she didn't have anything else to do when it was time to sit down at her desk, maybe she could give Holly some kindergarten work to do.

And that's exactly what she did after they were done making a hot chocolate. They went over to the desk, and Norma Jean grabbed the markers she had bought for the whiteboard on the wall.

Apparently in the spring, sometimes they wrote the date that they were changing pastures and different things that had to do with the cattle herds. Currently both whiteboards were completely blank, and so she slid the chair over, helped Holly to stand up on it, and showed her how to write a couple of letters.

Holly was already able to write her name, and so Norma Jean just went from there.

Norma Jean gave her a few things to work on on her own and went to her desk to get started on her own work.

She wouldn't have thought she would have enjoyed the company, but Holly chatted, jumping up and down from the chair, asking Norma Jean to check her work, and just generally giving a cheerful vibe to the small office. The day was overcast, and the little, cheerful presence was welcome. It was sad that the little girl's mom had gone off, and Norma Jean found herself wishing that there was something she could do.

Of course there wasn't. She couldn't make anyone want to come back, and she was probably too late anyway. Although with Miles's serious and somewhat dour personality, she could kind of understand why someone might leave. Women didn't really want a man they couldn't talk to, not that that made it okay to leave. Although, maybe he became like that because of his wife leaving.

Regardless, fifty-five minutes after Miles walked out the door, she told Holly it was time for them to make a hot chocolate.

"Of course, your dad said around an hour, so he might not be back exactly at an hour on the dot, but at least we'll be ready with his hot chocolate and it won't be completely cold."

"Okay," Holly said immediately, putting the lid back on her marker and setting it on the little tray before she got down from her chair and skipped over to Norma Jean's desk.

It turned out it was another fifteen minutes until Miles walked in. His hot chocolate was ready, and Norma Jean and Holly had made another cup for themselves.

"You can drink with us, Daddy," Holly said as she carefully carried his hot chocolate to him.

"After we're done drinking, you and I are going to go and make sure that everything is cleared off Peter's porch. I heard back from him, and he is going to be on his way home. Probably by dinnertime."

"Well. That's it?"

"I don't think he was hurt terribly. That broken leg was nasty, but other than that, he's a tough old bird."

She didn't think of Peter as a tough old bird, but she smiled at Miles's description.

"Well, I think Holly and I had a pretty good time while you were gone..." She looked at Holly, and Holly nodded her head up and down, making her ponytails swish back and forth. "She's always welcome to stay here if she wants to while you go and do whatever you need to make things ready for Peter."

"What do you think about that?" Miles said to Holly, and he seemed to be a little bit more relaxed. Maybe that was because Peter wasn't hurt badly. Maybe he had been worried this morning, and that's why he was quiet and seemed grumpy.

"Miss Norma Jean is teaching me my letters, so I won't be behind if I go to school next year."

"Is that the writing on the whiteboard over there? Those letters are so nice I thought it was Miss Norma Jean who was doing it."

"No. Me," Holly said with her chest puffed out real big.

"I see. Well, that was really nice of Miss Norma Jean to teach you, and you must be a pretty quick learner, because those are really nice letters."

"Thank you," Holly said, and her smile couldn't have been bigger.

Chapter 12

It was 5 o'clock when Peter made it in his house.

He had been so excited that morning, because he thought he'd be going home right away. But the hospital had fiddled and messed around, at least in Peter's eyes anyway, and it ended up being hours and hours later.

He was irritated, in pain, and feeling hung over from the drugs.

Having Sally beside him didn't even really help.

At least not as much as he would have thought it would have.

Although, she had been smiling and patient all day. Even when he had complained about the hospital staff being slow, promising him that he would be out by lunchtime and then barely making it by supper. She just smiled and shrugged.

It had prompted him to ask if anything ever bothered her.

She had tilted her head and said, "I hate it when people don't like me."

He had definitely taken note of that. After all, when someone could stay as patient and good-natured as Sally had all day, if there was something that bothered her, he definitely didn't want to engage in that behavior.

Regardless, he was finally home.

They'd ended up casting his leg, which was part of the reason it had taken so long. Normally, they didn't cast in the hospital, but for some reason, they'd done it with him.

Peter had gritted his teeth at each delay and tried to be kind, but he wasn't sure he was appreciating anything at this point in time.

Except, as Sally bent over him, adjusting a pillow on the couch and then straightening and asking him if he would like for her to cook supper, he smelled the scent that was uniquely hers, sweet and fluttery, it reminded him of smiles and happiness, and maybe it did ease his heart just a little.

"I don't want to take advantage of your kindness. You've already spent the day with me. And you do have another job."

"That reminds me. Franklin wanted you to call him. How about you go ahead and do that, and I'll look to see what you have in the kitchen and throw something to-gether for supper."

She waited for his nod before she turned.

She had been an angel all day. He was frustrated with his irritation. She didn't deserve to have him be grumpy with her.

One side of him said that he should cut himself some slack because anyone who was in as much pain as what he was should be expected to be a little bit grumpy. His head hurt, his ribs hurt, and his leg throbbed.

All that moving around had made everything hurt again, and the pain meds weren't touching it.

Regardless, he got his phone out, leaned his head back on the pillow that Sally had just adjusted, and called his brother.

"Hey, bro. You're alive?" Franklin said as Peter closed his eyes.

"I am. I can tell I'm not dead. There is not this much pain in the afterlife."

"Depends on which direction you go, or so I understand," Franklin said, not sounding like he had any pity for his little brother at all.

"Nice," Peter said. The very least Franklin could do would be to ask him how he was.

"How are you?"

Of course. He just needed to get to the right moment in the conversation. Peter took a deep breath and blew it out slowly. He needed to be patient and stop being such a grump.

"They sent me home, so I guess I'm not going to die today."

"Unless it's God's will."

"Wow. Thanks. So...encouraging."

"But it's probably not."

"That was not a good save."

"I tried."

"Sally said you wanted to talk to me?"

"Yeah. I was thinking that I can do Sally's job here. There's not much this time of year, and she can nurse you. I didn't say anything to her, just in case that wasn't the way you were going, but it kind of looked like it was at the beach party. I figured, since you're the reason that I'm happily married, I could do a little bit to nudge you in that direction." Franklin paused. "All right. My wife is over here with her hands on her hips giving me the evil eye. It was all her idea."

"Not bad. I believe that," Peter said, smiling. Franklin didn't have a clue about anything that related to matters of the heart, and Peter was not believing for one second that he was going to try to play matchmaker with his brother.

"I tried."

"Yeah, well, I wasn't buying it. So confession is good for the soul and all, but your lie was not working."

"All right, but the rest of it's true. Things are slow here, and I can easily handle the accounting for a bit. Sally has everything so well organized we probably could go without doing anything until we need to do our taxes in January."

"She's that good, huh?" Peter grinned a little. He believed it. She had been patient and kind, but those weren't her only good traits. She did seem to be well organized. He watched her as she moved around the kitchen, grateful for the open floor plan. She was graceful and had opened a few cupboards, stood in front of them for a bit, and then pulled a few things out, and then went to check the freezer.

"She is. And my wife wants me to give her away. That is ridiculous, but I'll do anything to keep my happy home." There was a little bit of scuffling going on from the sounds of things on the other end of the phone, and Peter just rolled his eyes. He wanted to be alone with Sally, wanted to have her as his accountant, wanted to spend time with her, but not like this.

He didn't want to be laid up, unable to do anything, having her wait on him hand and foot while he was a big grouch and in pain all the time. This wasn't the way to impress her.

"Well, I guess I appreciate it."

"You don't sound like it," Franklin stated.

"I just wish I wasn't laid out. I'm not really at my best."

"Women love that. They love to be the nurse, take care of you, hover around you doing all the nursing things."

"Whatever. You don't know anything about what women like. Stop trying to pretend you do. Go back to your numbers business." He was just joking, mostly. Although, it was true that Franklin didn't know anything about women. Well, not much. Maybe he learned a little since he got married.

"All right. Since you insist, I'll do that. Call me if you need anything."

"Wait."

"What?"

"Are you serious about not needing Sally?" He kept his voice low, and Sally didn't turn, so he hoped she didn't realize he was talking about her.

"Yeah. I was dead serious. She's great, and I don't really want to lose her, but my wife thinks it's a good idea, and typically when my wife has an idea, it's good."

"I see. All right."

They chatted for a bit more, and then Peter hung up. Thinking. About the time that Norma Jean figured out that Sally was in the house working, Norma Jean was going to come in and try to take over. Maybe it was the drugs talking, or maybe it was his grumpiness over the pain, but he could totally see that happening. And then Sally would be at the little office half a mile away from him, and Norma Jean would be in the house.

He hadn't figured anything out when there was a knock on the door and Sally called, "Come on in!"

"You have no idea who that could be. You might be inviting a serial killer into the house," he grumbled from the couch.

"Like a serial killer would knock," Sally said over her shoulder, rolling her eyes but smiling with that patient way she had that soothed his soul, even while it irritated him, mostly because he knew he wasn't nearly as patient as she was.

"Hey there. I'm not a serial killer, just in case I needed to say that before I was allowed in." Miles walked in the door, closing it behind him and nodding at Sally in the kitchen before he walked into the living room and stood with his hat in his hands in front of Peter.

Miles and Peter had been helping each other on their farms since Peter moved in. Miles had a bad split with his wife, and Peter, while not new to farming, had never had his own spread.

From what he could see, they helped each other, and both of them had been satisfied with their arrangement.

It wasn't going to be a fair split anymore.

"I can't stay long. Norma Jean is watching Holly over at the office."

"Norma Jean is watching Holly?"

"Yeah, Wanda didn't show up for her again."

"You didn't have to come," Peter said, although even as he spoke, he knew Miles pretty much did have to come.

Miles just lifted his brows. Both men knew Peter was wrong.

"Right," Peter said, irritated at himself again. "Sorry about that."

"It's hardly your fault someone left the gate open. I haven't figured that out. I was the last one through it."

"I wondered about that but had too many other things on my mind," mostly pain, but he didn't mention that, "to think about it."

"Yeah. It's been bugging me. I specifically remember putting Chester down, making him wait while I shut the gate and fastened it. I know it was latched securely. I... I'm not sure exactly what happened."

Peter supposed he would spend some time thinking about that, but it wasn't something that bothered him right now. Sure, whatever happened was the reason he was laid up, but it didn't change the fact that it had happened.

"I appreciate it. Sorry that Norma Jean had Holly all day."

Miles looked like he was surprised. "They actually hit it off." Miles fingered his hat. "I know you've been avoiding her some the last two weeks. Whatever happened, you didn't really say. I just know you made excuses to be outside and not in the office."

Peter looked away. He had. He'd managed not to complain about Norma Jean. He didn't want to go around bad-mouthing people. He didn't like spending time around people who never had anything nice to say about anyone and tried not to be that kind of person himself. But there hadn't been any question that he'd been avoiding Norma Jean.

"I wasn't going to let Holly stay with her, but Norma Jean did some letters with her, and they seem to be having a grand old time. She didn't even want to come here to see you."

Peter winced, ashamed. It galled a little that Holly liked Norma Jean better than she liked him. He wasn't upset about that exactly, but it made him feel bad.

Maybe he was being too hard on himself. It seemed like everything he did irritated him today.

"She actually seems like a nice girl," Miles said.

It made Peter pause. That was a lot more than Miles normally said. Ever since his wife walked out, he'd been soured on the female gender in general. It had been a whole year before his wife contacted him and demanded to be able to see her little girl. Like Miles had been keeping her from her or something. Which hadn't been the slightest bit true.

Peter thought about what Miles had just said—that Norma Jean seemed like a nice girl. A light bulb went on Peter's head. The first time, quite possibly, he had an idea about getting two people together in a romantic way.

Maybe desperation was the mother of invention, because if he did this, it would not only guarantee that Norma Jean wouldn't be in his house trying to push Sally out of a nursing position, but it might actually get two people together who...could be quite compatible.

"Do you think she would be able to learn to do some things on the farm?" Peter asked, trying to sound casual and not desperate.

"Um… What do you mean?" Miles said, his brows drawn down. "She's already doing the accounting. Do you mean ordering stuff?"

"No. Although, she could." A lot of times that involved being around the animals and just seeing what was needed. Making a list and having it be delivered. There were some things they ordered in bulk, and they had grain bins and bulk storage, but there were other things they didn't use a whole lot at a time and just ordered small quantities. Like minerals and certain types of grain that they fed to several of their older horses. Hog feed, since they only had three pigs, and bedding that they used with the horses when they needed to be on stall rest. Those types of things.

"I suppose she could. It's not that there's anything we do that's rocket science."

"Could she drive a tractor?"

"Probably. She apparently drives a car. There's one parked at the office, and I assumed it was hers."

Peter mentioned the color and make and model of her car.

"Yeah, that's it."

"Well, maybe she could...not take over for me but give you a hand. I will continue to pay her, since I'm putting you out."

"These things happen. I know you'd do the same for me. You don't have to feel like you owe me anything."

"No, really. I insist. If she's actually a help, she can go over with you and do the things that I have over there."

"Well, that might be possible, but if Wanda doesn't show up, I'll end up with Holly."

"I'm sure we can watch Holly here some. Sally is going to be around taking care of me, and she might be okay with Holly giving her a hand occasionally."

Miles glanced over his shoulder. "I think you might be a big enough handful for Sally. I wouldn't want to overburden her."

"It would not be a burden. Holly is as sweet of a child as I've ever seen. She makes everyone she meets smile."

Miles smiled a little, and Peter hid his satisfied smirk. Miles's one soft spot was Holly. He loved her beyond measure and would do anything for her.

"I suppose I could try. But the first time Norma Jean takes a tractor through the fence, I'm done."

"As long as it's your fence," Peter said, feeling better than he had the last hour. This could be the best idea he ever had.

Of course, it could end up exploding in his face and be the absolute worst idea he ever had too. It was hard to tell. Until a person actually lived through it, he couldn't really tell what the results were going to be. Especially when it came to matters of the heart.

"I'll go pick Holly up and see what Norma Jean says. She doesn't exactly look like the truck-driving type, but you can't always judge a book by its cover."

"You can never judge a book by its cover," Peter said, thrilled that it sounded like Miles was going to go along with his crazy scheme.

It wasn't a "crazy scheme." It was a help.

Help for both of them, possibly.

"All right. I'll call you later, let you know what I find out. And I'll tell you what Norma Jean says."

"All right."

They talked for a couple more minutes with Miles telling him what all he did that day. Although Peter paid attention, he wasn't really listening. He felt like he had solved his problems, and he might have actually done Miles a favor.

Still, in the back of his head he wondered about the gate. There had to be someone who had opened it after Miles closed it. Norma Jean might know. She was the only one who would have been around. She could tell if a car stopped in or anyone had gone into the office.

It wasn't long after Miles left that Sally dried her hands off on a dish towel as she made her way over. "I heard that. You do know I was in the kitchen the whole time?"

"That's pretty far away. Are you sure you heard as much as you thought you did?" Peter felt much better. Maybe just being still and letting the pain subside made his outlook more positive. Or maybe it was the smell coming from the kitchen. It certainly didn't smell like a hospital, although hospital food wasn't as bad as its rap.

"Are you going to try to get Norma Jean to work with Miles as well as the office?"

"I figured if I didn't, Norma Jean would be in here pushing you out, and as great of a nurse as I'm sure Norma Jean is, I'd rather have you."

Sally's smile showed that she was pleased, but rather than walking back in the kitchen, she perched on the edge of a chair. "Did I hear you say that someone opened the gate on purpose?"

Chapter 13

"We seem to meet here often," Miss Lana said as she walked up to Sally.

"Oh. Yeah, we do," Sally said, sounding preoccupied.

Lost in her own world after coming back from visiting Pierre and the three children he'd started to foster, Lana had been doing a lot of thinking. Pierre might have bitten off more than he could chew, and it was all her fault. He still wanted the same thing he'd wanted at the Beach Ball and Lana still wasn't sure what she should do.

But that wasn't a problem that could be solved now.

"I almost didn't recognize you there in the dark. But you're sitting the same way you were sitting the other day." Lana put her arms around herself. It was cold, and she didn't really want to sit outside in the sand, but it seemed that Sally might need a listening ear. Her best friend, Norma Jean, wasn't the kind of person who typically listened and gave good advice. While Lana knew there were reasons for that, Sally had been very tight-lipped about her and hadn't done any complaining the last time they talked. Which Lana really admired.

Still, the fact remained that Sally could use a friend. So, she tipped up her chin, trying to tell herself that she wasn't that cold, and her bones weren't that old, and her muscles weren't that sore, and she settled down in the sand beside Sally.

"Is it okay if I sit a while?" she asked after she was down. She didn't want Sally to tell her no, so she sat down first. It was an old trick she learned from her mom. Of course, it wasn't a trick she used much, just when she thought that someone might not want to bother her but needed a shoulder.

"Of course. I actually appreciate it when I get to talk to you. Whenever you come by, it just feels like having a mom."

That made Lana's heart warm, and her body wasn't as cold. A warm heart was better than a warm body. She wanted to give off motherly feelings. She wanted to do what good she could in the world. She didn't have a whole lot of time left. Sure, she was only in her fifties, but she had so many things she wanted to do, so many people who needed her help, she didn't want to waste even one breath without using it to be a blessing if she could.

"Aww, that just made me smile," Lana said, putting her arm around Sally just like she would have if she were one of her daughters.

To her surprise, Sally leaned into her and laid her head on her shoulder.

"Are you gonna tell me what you're thinking about?" Lana said after a few moments of sitting in comfortable silence.

"Peter said he thought someone opened the gate on purpose."

"The gate that allowed the bull out that charged him?"

"Yes."

"That was you?"

"Oh no! I wasn't there at all that day. It definitely wasn't me."

"You're worried it might have been Norma Jean?"

"Peter insisted that it probably wasn't. He said lots of people stop at the office, and that when he got a chance to talk to Norma Jean, he'd ask if she could remember if she saw something that morning and see if they could figure it out. Actually, he thought that maybe Norma Jean would put two and two together and go to Miles or to Peter, and let them know who she suspected."

"I don't know that Norma Jean's been around the farm long enough to even think about that," Lana said thoughtfully.

"That's assuming it wasn't her."

"And you're worried it was?"

"Yeah."

"Do you have any evidence to back up your fear?"

"Not really. Just... I know that Norma Jean will stop at nothing to get what she wants. Well, I guess I shouldn't say that. Norma Jean isn't a mean person. She doesn't want to see people hurt. But I can see her thinking that opening the gate would somehow bring Peter to her. And Peter has admitted that he was trying to avoid her. So, I'm just putting together what I know about Norma Jean with what Peter said."

"Did you express your fears to Peter?"

"No. How could I?"

Lana didn't say anything, just lightly rubbed her hand up and down Sally's arm.

"It's just speculation. I wouldn't want to get him upset with her, especially if it turned out to be nothing. I just... I'm just afraid I might be right."

"And you could be. But maybe this is what Norma Jean needs in order to learn a lesson."

"But I hate to see Peter suffering because Norma Jean needed to learn a lesson."

"Maybe there's something for Peter to learn as well," Lana said, and then she added, "and you're not God, right? I mean, I know you know you're not. He allowed this? Right?"

"Yes. But it could have been prevented."

"It's true that God doesn't save us from our stupidity at times."

Sally snorted. "You can say that again."

"But I can kinda see that God might be working in a way that you might not have thought of."

"And how's that?"

"Well, Norma Jean has a few lessons to learn."

"True."

"And so do you."

"That's for sure."

"And maybe, maybe God had that happen to Peter because he knew that Peter would ask you to nurse him, and you and

Peter will be spending a good bit of time together. Which, if I recall correctly, you might have been hoping for the last time we spoke."

"I hadn't thought of it that way."

"I'm just asking. You know, God can work everything out for your good and His glory, even accidents that aren't really accidents, if we allow it. Now, Peter will probably have pain for the rest of his life, broken bones often do that. And he might have issues with his concussion or other things we don't even know about. But those might be things that God wants Peter to learn to deal with. And He just used this as the vehicle for Peter to be in a position where God wanted him. I mean, do we believe that all things work together for good?"

"All things. As in everything. That's a good point. Even accidents that happen on purpose can turn out for our good. Even things that feel like they shouldn't happen, like Peter being in pain, I see what you're saying. I just... You know you want someone to blame. You want someone to take responsibility."

"And Norma Jean should, if she was the one who opened the gate. Or whoever did. If it was on purpose especially, but taking the blame, taking responsibility, and facing up to what you did are all good things. And I wouldn't say that she shouldn't do it. But I am saying that you don't want to spend your life bitter and angry because something happened to you. You want to accept the fact that God allowed it."

"Right. I'm glad you said that, because while I don't think I am upset to the point of bitterness, I do think that if Norma Jean opened that gate, she needs to... I don't know."

"You need to let God handle what lesson that she needs to learn, right?"

"Sometimes if we're not punished, we keep doing things. I guess that's what my problem is with forgiveness. I feel like people should be punished."

"I can see that. I mean, a parent punishes their child so that they don't continue to do wrong things, but it's not an adult's responsibility to punish another adult."

"Unless they committed a crime."

"True. Although, I feel like Christians can say that if they feel like the person is remorseful and regretful, that there doesn't need to be a punishment. God will take care of the vengeance. After all, you can't take the accident back."

"True. I guess... If the government requires punishment, it's okay. But it's not up to a Christian to punish other Christians?"

"You might be getting in a little bit over my head." Lana knew there was a line there, but she just wasn't sure where it was.

"Mine too. Because I keep thinking of Old Testament law, and there were definitely punishments for crimes. But

Christians are supposed to forgive. We're not supposed to exact vengeance. That's supposed to be up to the Lord."

"Those are the things that we know. Things I can say for certain."

"It's not really my position to make a decision anyway. That's Peter's place."

"If I'm not mistaken, you're going to have a good bit of influence over Peter."

Sally huffed out a bit of a laugh, and Lana squeezed her. "I don't know. I do really love spending time with him. He is...funny even when he's in pain. In fact, he seemed to make a concerted effort to not be grumpy. I kept thinking that if I hurt as bad as he must, I would hardly be fit to be around, but he kept cracking jokes and making me laugh. Which I hated because then when he laughed, he hurt his ribs, and he would groan almost every time."

"Men. They'll do anything to make a girl laugh."

"Really? Any girl?"

"No. If you've got a good man, he's only concerned about making one girl laugh."

"I think Peter is a good man."

"I think you've got yourself a good man too."

"Oh, he's not mine," Sally was quick to point out.

"You don't think so?"

"No."

"He's letting you take care of him, isn't he?"

"Well, yeah. So far. But he doesn't really have anyone else."

"Oh, Peter could hire someone, so could Franklin. Neither one of those boys are struggling for money. And there are plenty of ladies in town who wouldn't mind going out and earning some extra."

"If you say so."

"I do."

They didn't say anything for a while, and Lana didn't figure they needed to. Sally seemed like she figured out the issue with Norma Jean, and Lana realized that maybe she wasn't quite as cold as what she thought she was going to be.

Or maybe it was just sitting with a friend. Daughter almost.

That was the nice thing about Strawberry Sands, everyone was so close to everyone else.

She thought again about her visit and the different things Pierre told her that evening after they put the children to bed.

They'd walked out of the lighthouse to talk, since there wasn't much privacy inside. It had been a long time since she walked on the beach with a man, and she enjoyed it more than what she wanted to admit.

Pierre hadn't seemed to notice that she was beside him, since he was so wrapped up in the issues with his kids.

He'd gone from being deeply invested in his business to deeply invested in the children who were in his care. He didn't even know for how long. Their parents were still trying to figure things out so they could get them back.

So many issues and so many problems. Lana wished she could help, and she knew of several ways. But they would require her leaving the place that she loved and the town that she lived in all her life.

That wasn't her plan. She planned on dying in Strawberry Sands.

Sometimes God had other plans, some of which involved moving a lady who was set in her ways, happy where she was, but was needed somewhere else.

Lord, I want to submit to Your will and Your plan, but these old bones don't really want to move anywhere.

She knew he heard her, but just like she and Sally had been talking about, she also knew that God knew what was best, and sometimes He moved in a way that wasn't what she wanted but was exactly what she needed. It happened all the time throughout her life, and she was afraid that maybe now was one of those times.

But she didn't want to be too down, because there were a lot of bright spots on the horizon. The three children were one of them, and Pierre was another. He was a good man. A man that if Lana were younger, she might have been able to fall in love with.

Chapter 14

"I think you're ready," Rodney said as he turned from hanging up the last of the harnesses and leaned over top of Ashes's broad back.

"I don't know. I don't feel ready," Becky said, a sour mixture of fear and pain splashing against her heart. It wasn't really that she didn't feel like she was ready to handle Cinders and Ashes, Ronnie's big Percheron team that he used to give people carriage rides on the beach. She actually loved driving them, loved working with them, loved everything about it.

The problem was, she didn't want to do it without Rodney. And, the fear was that he would go to college and find a girl and fall in love with her. And then, Becky would be left behind in Strawberry Sands, taking care of his horses, giving carriage rides, and basically running his business, until he brought his new love back, and kicked Becky out.

She'd been kicked out before. Maybe not in so many words, but her mother hadn't wanted her, her dad hadn't wanted her, and she had too many foster families to name who hadn't wanted her. She knew all about how it felt to be kicked aside. It was kind of what she'd come to expect out of her life.

And, her way of dealing was to suck it up and pretend she didn't care.

It was just really hard this time, because Rodney had been the one person in her life who seemed to like her no matter what. He'd been there for everything, and he seemed to see something in her that no one else had seen.

Now he was leaving.

"Hey. What's wrong?" he asked, his brow furrowing, the smile slowly slipping off his face.

He ducked around, underneath Ashes's neck, and stood in front of her as she stood with her back toward Cinders, leaning against her flank.

"Nothing."

"Nothing?" he asked, with his brow raised. His finger came out, and he lifted her chin. "Why do you have that belligerent look on your face, if there's nothing wrong?"

"I don't have my belligerent look on," she said, sounding snotty but unable to help it, as she crossed her arms over her chest.

"What's this?" He pointed to her arms which she promptly uncrossed and dropped down to her sides, but not before he chuckled.

"Spit it out, Beckpet. What's the problem?"

"There's no problem."

He just stood there, his brows raised, his finger holding her chin up.

The stable was warm, and the sound of the horses munching their hay was soothing and relaxing. Becky didn't notice that, or the familiar scents that felt like home to her, or anything else. She just didn't seem to be able to look away from Rodney as the amusement in his eyes fell away, and something else took its place.

She admired what he had done. He had experienced unimaginable tragedy when his parents had passed away, and he almost slipped into something wrong and bad, but with the help of some of the men in the town, he turned his life around. He'd become amusing and fun, and a hard worker. He managed to run a profitable business, which he was passing on to her.

Except she didn't want him to do that, because it meant he was going away.

Why couldn't she be honest with him?

"Becky? You know you can tell me whatever it is."

"If you know so much, you tell me."

She lifted her chin in the air. His finger followed, and it seemed like his thumb brushed lightly over her cheek, or maybe she imagined it, because the touch was there and then it was gone just that fast.

"So there's some boy you like at school, and he doesn't like you back. And it's made you unhappy."

"No." He had it partly right. There was a boy. But he wasn't in school. He was standing in front of her.

"Don't you trust me?" he asked, softly, and it was a question, not an insistence that she had to. He never demanded her trust. He always appreciated it when she gave it, but he didn't demand it when she didn't.

"I do."

"Then tell me."

Was that the key? If she trusted him with her safety, could she trust him with her feelings?

But what was she going to say? Could she tell him that she loved him? He'd laugh. He'd say she was too young to know whether she loved someone or not.

She was sixteen. That wasn't too young.

She found she couldn't. It wasn't that she didn't trust him. It was that she was scared to death that he would laugh at her for telling him how she felt about him, and tell her that she should find someone her own age, that he was going to college and he would find someone who was competent and beautiful and smart and everything that Becky wasn't.

Still, he didn't move, and so she said, "There's a boy who wants to kiss me. But I don't know how to kiss."

There. It was kind of true. There was a boy at school who wanted to kiss her. He'd been bugging her at school for a while, and even caught her when she'd been walking across the parking lot on an errand for the athletic director. She'd ducked around him, and gotten away easily, but the idea of kissing him made her want to throw up.

Rodney, on the other hand, certainly didn't elicit any feelings like that in her. Far from them.

"Really?" His tone was... She wasn't sure. Was he annoyed?

"Yeah. I guess I could, but what am I supposed to do?"

She was trying to play it cool, like they were just talking about it and it didn't mean anything, but that wasn't really the way she felt.

"You're supposed to kiss him back."

"And how does that work?"

A breath huffed out of his nose, and maybe one corner of his mouth lifted up, and this time she was sure his thumb rubbed over her cheek because it wasn't just a light touch that she might have imagined, but it stayed on her cheek, and rubbed a little circle there.

"I think that's one of those things that you figure out as you're doing it," he said, and his words were low and murmured with a rumbling sound that made her stomach clench and hold on tight to her rib cage like it was bracing for a fall.

"Really? So, you'll help me learn how to drive your horses, but you're not going to teach me how to kiss?"

"I didn't realize that was what you were asking me to do," he said, and his eyes had gone from amused, to some kind of smoky heat that made her toes curl.

"Yeah. You said you'd help me with anything. I'm waiting for you to help."

There, she all but asked him to kiss her. Of course, the clinical, let me teach you how to kiss kind of kiss was not exactly the kind of kiss she wanted from him.

She wanted more. Everything, to be honest.

Her mouth was completely dry as he stared down at her, and she thought for a moment that he was going to tell her no. Then his head moved closer.

Her fingers balled into fists at her sides and she waited, holding her breath.

"How old are you?" he asked softly.

"Sixteen. You know it."

"Yeah. I do." He swallowed hard, and his eyes, which had been holding hers, dropped to her lips.

He let out a shaky breath.

"If you still haven't kissed anyone when I graduate from college, I'll come back and give you all the kissing lessons you want." He took another shaky breath, then his thumb touched her cheek once more, before his hand dropped and he stepped back. His voice wasn't quite back to normal, but it was louder as he said, "You're too young right now, and I'm not kissing you and then leaving for four years." He grinned a little. "And I don't think you really want to anyway. Regardless, I'm not kissing you until I graduate from college and come back home. And I don't think you can wait that long so you'll get lessons from someone else."

"You'll be back before that," she said, unable to think of anything else to say over the bitter disappointment that backed up like bile in her throat.

"It's possible. Cord Stryker out in North Dakota has some things he wants me to do, and Griff thinks I should work out west for a while so that's probably a good idea."

"Why haven't you been talking to me about this?"

"Because every time I see you we talk about horses." His lips flattened. "Plus, you have a life with your family now. You have parents, you're with your sister, and you have school. You don't need to hear about me."

She wanted to hear about him. She wanted to know everything there was to know about him, but if she said that, she was afraid she was going to start crying.

"I'll wait for four years. Just because you said I couldn't," she said, her eyes narrow.

There was a look that flashed across his face, almost a look of triumph, like he knew that was what she was going to say, but was gone so fast she couldn't be sure.

"No you won't," he said, smirking at her.

Whatever spell had been between them was broken, and she found that instead of wanting to kiss him, she wanted to stomp her foot and march away angrily.

"Oh yes I will. You just wait and see if I don't."

"All right. I will."

"It's a deal," she said, holding out her hand.

"Sorry. It hardly seems fair that you're the only one waiting. So, if you wait, I will too."

She hadn't been expecting that, and she could hardly contain herself. She didn't have to worry about him finding some other girl who was better than she was. He just said he would wait for her.

"All right. It's a bet." She gave him a triumphant look as she held her hand out, and he took it and they shook.

In four years, if she could wait that long, Rodney, the boy who had saved her, would kiss her.

Four years seemed like forever.

Chapter 15

"I can't believe you like this game," Peter grumbled as he stared at the board of Chinese checkers. They each played three colors, and the middle of the board was packed solid.

"I love it. There's so much strategy." Sally knew her words were going to irritate him, not in a bad way, just in a fake grumble kind of way. And he didn't disappoint her.

"How can you have a strategy? There aren't any ways to move. There are no jumps, all you can do is move one marble one spot, and by the time I'm ready to jump it, you'll have one of your marbles in the spot I opened up!"

"And I don't see how that's a bad thing," Sally teased.

Peter had been doing well over the past two weeks, and they'd gotten into the habit of playing games in the afternoon after lunch, before he took a nap.

He didn't actually say that he was going to nap, but she would pretend to stand up and stretch and be tired and she would go over and sit down on the couch, and he would sit down on the recliner, and two minutes later, he'd be snoring.

It had become very normal.

But first, she had to beat him in Chinese checkers, which she had been doing on a regular basis since they started playing the day after he came home from the hospital.

"You know, if we keep doing this, I'm going to beat you someday."

"All right," she said.

"You don't have to be so agreeable."

"You say that at least seventy times a day. You know, you don't have to tell me that all the time."

"Maybe if I say it often enough, you'll start listening to me."

"Maybe I'm happy with myself the way I am," she said, although that wasn't the slightest bit true. She could see all the ways that she needed to improve, and there were plenty more that she couldn't see, she was sure.

"Hey! There's a good move," Peter said, and he jumped two spots with his black marble.

"Wow," Sally said before she picked up her white marble and jumped five.

She moved her other two colors and then put her chin on her hand while she waited for him to move.

"You know, if you weren't such a good cook, I think I would fire you."

"Because I beat you at Chinese checkers? That doesn't sound very professional."

"I never said anything about being a professional."

"Your brother told me you are a professional."

"I didn't know there was such a thing as a professional farmer."

"You're pretty good at business. I think that makes you a professional."

"No. Being good at business is not hard. Being honest in business is hard."

"If you say so." But she liked that. She liked the fact that he differentiated between being good and being honest. Or the fact that he felt that being honest was more important than being good.

"So have you talked to Norma Jean at all?" he asked after a bit.

"Why? Do you miss her?" Norma Jean had come in every day for the first four days. But every time, Miles had come in for her and taken her back out.

"No. You know I don't," Peter said, moving each one of his colors one spot.

"I'd like to be a fly on the wall, listening to Norma Jean and Miles. There's...some sort of attraction going on, but they seem to not like each other."

"It is a bit weird," Peter said, but there was no interest in his voice at all. Sally knew he cared for his friend and wanted him and Norma Jean to be happy, but what happened in their relationship wasn't of any interest at all to Peter.

His eyes lit up when they talked about cows, and they talked about the farm as well.

Sally also thought his eyes lit up when he talked to her, but maybe that was just something she wanted to see.

She moved again, this time jumping almost the entire way around the board to get her green marble in the very bottom home spot.

"How did you see that?" Peter said.

"That's what I do while you're playing. I try to find jumps for my marbles. I told you that."

"Why would you think of going backward in order to go forward?" Peter muttered as he looked at his own marbles, moving them back before he moved two one space and found jumps for his third.

"I don't know. I just do it in my head." Sally knew the more they played, the better he would get. He was already a lot better than what he had been. She had a huge advantage because she loved playing Chinese checkers and had played all the time with Aunt Wilma before she had gotten too sick to play.

"If I ask you something, will you not think I'm a terrible person?" Peter said as he stared at the board, not glancing at her to see what her reaction was.

It was a good thing, because her mouth opened, and she had trouble closing it.

"You know I'm not going to think you're a terrible person."

"Well, I just keep having this thought that I can't get rid of."

"All right, I'm curious now."

"Well, it's about Norma Jean."

"Okay?" Sally forgot about looking for jumps as she looked at him across the board. Her heart clenched. Maybe he decided he liked her after all. Sally held her breath.

"Do you think she might have opened the gate on purpose?" He asked the question while he looked at the board, and then he lifted his head, meeting her eyes.

Oh boy. Sally didn't know what to say. She wanted to tell the truth. Which was that she thought it was very likely that Norma Jean might have opened the gate.

"It makes me feel mean to think she might have done that. But I... I know she manipulated other things, just so that she could get me to spend time with her. I told you about her asking me a million questions, but I didn't tell you that she unplugged the coffee maker and asked me to come fix it. She flushed a wad of toilet paper down the toilet and caused it to overflow."

"I didn't know about those things. But I guess I've been thinking about it."

"Miles said he spoke with her, and she said that there wasn't anyone else in the office that morning. She doesn't know that we think that the gate was deliberately opened, since Miles had closed it."

"Maybe he didn't close it right?" Sally said, and she couldn't help the fact that her voice sounded hopeful.

"Well, Miles has closed a lot of gates. I'd say he knows how to do it correctly. But more than that, he specifically told me that he remembered bringing Chester through and putting him down, which is a common practice with cattle dogs. He just made him lie down while he shut the gate. And he said he remembered shutting it and latching it."

"Oh."

"I know. She's your friend, and you don't want there to be any bad blood between you two. And that's part of the reason I hesitated saying anything to you."

"Well, you know I would say something if Norma Jean told me that she did it on purpose. I wouldn't hesitate to tell you."

"No. I know. I just wondered if you thought that that was something that she might do."

Sally forgot all about the checkers and stared at the board without seeing anything. She couldn't lie. But she didn't want to throw her friend under the bus.

She also didn't want to protect her friend at the expense of someone else.

It was a moral dilemma, and she wasn't sure what was exactly right.

"I don't want to admit it, but I can see her doing it. I'm...not saying she did, just saying it wouldn't be out of character."

"I thought as much," Peter said, and he didn't sound very happy.

"I guess I suspected, but when I think about it, I wonder if it matters."

"Of course it matters. My leg will heal up, but I'll probably always have issues with it. And a concussion, even one, can have permanent repercussions."

"God could make those things not be an issue?"

"Of course. But if Norma Jean hadn't opened the gate, they wouldn't be an issue either."

"Right," Sally said slowly. "But it doesn't matter whether Norma Jean opened the gate or not, God is in control either way, right?"

Peter stared at her, anger still on his features, but slowly the tension drained out of his shoulders.

"Why are you always right?" he asked, and he didn't sound very happy about it.

"I'm sorry," she said softly. She hated this. She didn't want to make anyone feel bad. Just like she didn't necessarily want to beat him at Chinese checkers. But she wasn't going to play anything less than her best game, just to keep Peter happy or to allow him to win. And she couldn't not say things, if they were the correct things, even though they might not be what he wanted to hear.

"I didn't mean that in a bad way," he said, gazing across the board at her, concern on his features.

"It kinda sounded bad," she said dryly.

"I'm sorry," he said.

"No. I shouldn't let it bother me, just sometimes... I know I should just keep my mouth shut. But I sometimes say things that, while they might be accurate, they don't always help."

"You did. It did help. I shouldn't have teased you about always being right."

"Sometimes people say I am a little too perfect. Or am a little too...easy. They don't understand that I've worked hard to be that way. Because I feel like that's the way the Lord wants me to be. Not perfect, but kind. Not quick to be angry."

"Wherefore, my beloved brethren, let every man be swift to hear, slow to speak, slow to wrath."

"Yeah. That doesn't come naturally to anyone, I don't think."

"Nor does being kind to people who aren't kind to you."

"Exactly."

"Nor does...forgiving people when you feel like they don't deserve it," he said, and there was bitterness in his voice but also guilt.

"I don't want to guilt you into forgiveness."

"You're not. You just opened my eyes and made me see that maybe it wasn't all Norma Jean. I wanted to point the finger at her. I wanted to say she was a terrible person. I want to hear you tell me that it was totally within the realm of possibility that she did exactly what I thought she did. And that would justify me getting angry and pressing charges."

"But?" she prompted when he stopped.

"But maybe seeing you and how you treated her, there was a part of me that said she deserves to have someone who actually holds her accountable for her actions. But what I failed to see was maybe I needed to grow, rather than worrying about making sure everyone else gets what they deserve."

"Forgive."

"Exactly, and there I was trying to excuse myself."

"That doesn't have anything to do with me being annoying because I'm perfect," she said, using her fingers to do air quotes, because she knew she was not perfect. Far from it.

"That's not annoying. It's convicting." He grinned at her. "There's a difference."

"A very fine difference apparently." She meant it as a joke, to lighten the air between them, because his compliment was making her uncomfortable. She didn't see herself that way. More like someone who needed work—a lot of work—and was not an example for anyone.

"You want to be around people who make you better. Every time I'm around you, I learn something, or I get better. Except for Chinese checkers." He wrinkled his nose up and squinted at the board. The backlog in the middle had mostly eased out, but he still had marbles that were still in their starting position, and Sally had marbles that were sitting there waiting to go into those slots. "Thank you. Thank you for being someone I can look up to and who forces me to take a look at myself and realize I need to be better."

She stared at the board, feeling bad.

"Compliments are supposed to make you smile," he teased, moving just a little, as though trying to catch her eye. She didn't look at him though, although she knew she had to answer him. To at least explain why she was acting so oddly.

"Sally?" he prompted.

"I'm sorry. I... I just don't feel like I deserve a compliment like that. I mean, I guess sometimes I do act the way I should, but I feel like I fail more than I succeed, and that I'm a terrible example for anyone. And then, if you only knew the things I thought. I'm not someone who should be anyone that people look up to."

"I think we all have thoughts like that. No one is perfect. And maybe you misunderstood, because I wasn't telling you you were perfect."

"No, I didn't misunderstand." She smiled.

"Good, because I wouldn't want you to get confused." He moved one of his marbles and then looked back up at her. "But it's okay to say thank you. You don't have to say anything else."

"Even when I feel like I don't deserve it?"

"I guess if you felt like you deserved it, I probably wouldn't be saying it. Because it wouldn't be true."

She tilted her head and then huffed out a laugh. "I guess that makes sense."

"I see what you're saying, you don't want me to think more highly of you than what you are, because you're afraid..." His voice trailed off like he wasn't sure what she might be afraid of. But she knew.

"I'm afraid that you'll be disappointed when you find out that I'm not as good as what you seem to think I am."

His smile was gentle. "I don't think you need to worry about that."

"Maybe you're saying that because I don't gloat when I beat you, and quite soundly," she said as she jumped her last marble into the last spot.

His were still scattered all over the board, and she lifted her brows, looking first at the board and then at him.

"Man. How do you do that?"

"You know what? I just realized you were giving that compliment because you were trying to take my attention off the game so that you could try to win."

"That was my entire strategy. Busted."

They laughed together as they cleaned up the board, and then she put the game away as he slowly made his way over to the recliner where he normally took his rest.

She knew he was frustrated with how slowly time was going by, that he was stuck in the house not doing anything while Miles was out doing most of the work.

She appreciated the fact that he wasn't grumpy and sour about it.

Maybe she should have told him. Maybe she should return the compliment when he gave her one. Next time, she would do better. Or maybe she'd compliment him first. She smiled at the thought.

Chapter 16

"So I'm getting the cast off today, right, doc?" Peter sat on the edge of the chair, uncomfortable. The way most of his life had been since his accident. It was difficult to find any position that wasn't awkward with such a huge cast on his leg.

"Unfortunately," the doctor began, and Peter's heart dropped.

He had come into this appointment with all the optimism in the world. The cast had been on for four weeks. At two weeks he hadn't expected to have the doctor say that he was healed. But four weeks? He'd always been quick to recover. He didn't see why it should be any different now.

"No. I had considered going with a smaller cast, to give you more mobility. But I think we need to keep this bigger one on, and continue to restrict your movements. That will allow the bone a little more time to fuse together."

"You're kidding." Peter's words came out in a whisper. He didn't want the doctor to see how upset he was, but it was hard to hide. Sally had been doing an excellent job of taking care of him, and he'd been finding himself thinking about her more and more. And he thought she felt the same way about him. But he didn't want to move forward in their relationship, not as long as he couldn't even go out and feed the dog without help. It was all he could do to get himself to the restroom. He didn't want to pursue a relationship when he was so incompetent.

"No. Unfortunately I'm not. When you're a child, your bones are growing, and a broken bone often doesn't take long at all to heal. But, as an adult, bone growth slows, and healing takes more time."

The doctor didn't look like he was done speaking, and Peter didn't say anything. Not that he wanted to. What more was there to say? The doctor couldn't make his bones grow any faster.

"With your concussion, and now the broken leg, this is going to change your life."

"How so?" Peter asked, wondering if there was more bad news.

"Well, studies have shown that even one concussion increases your risk for a variety of other issues on down the road. And, often when you break a bone, it's something that you feel for the rest of your life. Maybe when a storm comes in, and the barometer drops. You're getting older, and these are going to be some of the aches and pains that are going to accompany you as you do it."

The doctor might have said a few more things, Peter was too annoyed to notice, and then he clapped Peter on the shoulder, and Peter hobbled out.

Sally looked up as he came into the waiting room. She had driven him to his appointment, since he couldn't even drive.

Talk about discouraging.

He knew she was concerned about him as they rode home. Normally he was fairly jovial, enjoyed joking, and tried to make her laugh. It had become one of his favorite passtimes since he had broken his leg and they'd spent so much time together, but he couldn't even find it in himself to want to make her smile.

"I'm going to assume from the way you looked the entire way home that nothing the doctor said was good." Sally finally said that as she pulled into the driveway to his house.

He heard her, but he didn't want to answer. But, that wasn't the way he should treat someone who had been so good to him. And whether or not Sally cared about him was not a question. The only question he had was how much.

"Yeah. Just basically I'm going to be feeling this for the rest of my life. It makes me angry that someone left the gate open. And instead of them suffering, it's going to be me." He knew he sounded bitter and angry, but that's because he was.

Sally opened her mouth, but he put a hand up. "I know. I know. I know exactly what you're going to say. You're going to say that God allowed it, so therefore I should just accept that it's coming from

God, and figure out what lessons I need to learn, and just decide to be happy. Blah blah blah."

Her mouth closed. He felt bad. His words had not been kind, and his tone more than anything showed his aggravation.

He couldn't seem to help himself.

He pressed his lips together, but couldn't bring himself to say anything else. Anger and bitterness bubbled inside of him, like poison, nasty and hot. If he could prove that it was Norma Jean who left the gate open, he'd press charges. He wanted to punish her, and ruin her life the way she'd ruined his.

He struggled to get inside, brushing off Sally's gentle, helping hands.

She served him supper without saying anything, and he sat solemnly on the couch as she moved around the kitchen, cleaning it up, washing dishes, and putting everything away the way she had done for four weeks now. He didn't exactly breathe a sigh of relief as she walked upstairs to her room after asking if he needed anything. He said, "No," and it sounded just as nasty as the last words he'd spoken to her.

Why? Why couldn't he be nice? Why couldn't he push these feelings aside and just do what he knew to be right, and overcome what he felt like doing, which was to be unkind the way he'd been.

Lord. What's wrong with me?

He wanted to do right. He wanted to please the Lord, but he also wanted to do it with a whole body. Not a body that was crippled and sore and prone to strokes and brain bleeds and tumors because of someone's stupidity.

Are you upset because you didn't get your way? I thought you wanted to submit to My will?

That question brought him up short. That was exactly what the problem was. It didn't really have anything to do with his body being whole. It had more to do with him expecting that he deserved to have a pain free life. That he had expectations about what was going to happen in his life and they were not going to be met anymore.

He sat with his Bible open in his lap, but he didn't see the words. He just thought about that question. And the idea of him acting like a petulant child, pitching a fit because he didn't get what he wanted.

He typically had trouble getting comfortable to go to sleep, and that night was no different. At two AM, he finally got up and hobbled to the restroom, not because he needed to go as much as he just needed to get up and move around. Nothing felt relaxing and sleep was elusive.

He had settled back down on the couch when Sally's voice came down the stairs.

"Peter?" He could hear her footsteps, and the stairs creaking as she slowly descended.

"Are you okay?"

"Sorry. I didn't mean to get you up," he said, and his voice sounded defeated.

"It's okay. That's what I'm here for."

"You're not supposed to be my twenty-four, seven nursemaid. I'm a man, not an invalid."

At least he didn't want to be. What if he was? What if he had broken his neck in the accident, and someone had to take care of him every day for the rest of his life? Would God give him grace to accept that?

But that wasn't what happened. What happened to him was far less bad, and yet...he was still upset about it.

"I know. But, I want to help if I can."

"I'm sorry I was so mean to you earlier," he said, feeling contrite to the very tips of his toes. She hadn't deserved to bear the brunt of his frustration.

"I understand that you didn't hear what you wanted to with the doctor. I was available as a scapegoat for your disappointment."

"Yeah. That was very childish of me."

"For the most part, you've handled this with aplomb. I think you're allowed to be childish once in a while."

"No. Not when it hurts someone I...have become so fond of."

"You're fond of me?" Sally asked, laughter in her voice. "How fond?"

"I think you know."

"I wasn't so sure about it today."

"A bad mood doesn't change how I feel."

"It's hard to see that when you're on the receiving end of that bad mood."

"I'm sorry."

"It's okay. I don't think anyone expects you to be perfect. And I understand that it has to be annoying and frustrating to not be able to do what you want."

"That's just it. As I was thinking about that this evening after you went to bed, I realized that... That's the way my life is supposed to be. Just calm acceptance from God of whatever He wants to give me. And, I don't have a problem with that calm acceptance as long as the things that He gives me are what I want.

The problem comes when he gives me trials that I don't feel I deserve."

"Ah. That's wise."

"I was really angry at Norma Jean for a while. I wanted to press charges. I wanted to ruin her life the way it feels like she's ruined mine, but that's not really showing calm acceptance of my trial from the Lord, is it?"

"No. It's not."

"And I started to think that maybe I needed this trial."

"Needed?" Sally asked, as she slipped a little closer through the dark and knelt down beside the couch, her hand on his forearm.

He put his other hand over top of hers, and their fingers threaded together. Hers were slender and a little cool, and they felt delicate and small.

"Yeah. I needed the reminder that happiness is a choice. I... I can choose to be bitter and angry, to allow myself to feel like I deserve better. That someone else deserves to suffer because I'm suffering, or, I can choose forgiveness, and happiness."

"Maybe I need to listen too."

"You're always cheerful."

"But I'm not always happy. I... I forget that it's not the job of the people around me to make me happy, but it's my job to choose to be happy."

"Yeah. I have that expectation too. That other people should do what I want them to do in order for me to be happy, but that's not what life is about. It's about accepting what God has given you, and being happy anyway."

"That's true." She was quiet for a minute, and then she said softly, "We're talking like everything that God does ends up being some painful trial that we have to go through. But sometimes He really does give us what our hearts want."

"Like forced proximity with the girl I have a crush on?"

"Is that all this is?" Sally asked, and from the dim glow of the light above the kitchen sink, he could see her face turn up to his. "Just a crush?"

"It feels like a lot more."

"To me too."

"I wondered how you felt."

"You can ask." Her lips pulled up, and her teeth sparkled. "I think normally women don't have too much trouble talking about how they feel."

"How do you feel about me, Sally?"

"I admire you. I appreciate the fact that you're more interested in what God wants than what you want. I love your character and your convictions. And I love that you're trying to take something hard that's happened to you and turn it into something that you can learn a lesson from."

"Those aren't feelings," he said, closing his eyes as her breath fanned over his face. He wasn't sure when she moved closer, but he certainly wasn't going to complain about it. He took one hand, and trailed it down the side of her face.

"True," she said, her voice soft. "I feel...like I might be falling in love with you."

"That's how I feel too," he said, wanting to say more, but not wanting to be unable to even walk when he asked her if they could have an exclusive relationship. That's what he wanted. A relationship that culminated in a lifetime commitment. Was that too much too soon? He wanted to move forward, didn't want to be stuck in limbo, but...

He lost his train of thought as her face moved closer and her lips trailed over his cheek.

"Really?" she breathed.

It took a little bit to figure out what she was questioning him about. Falling in love. That was it.

"Yeah. I love you. Is that crazy?"

"No. It's perfect."

Her lips moved from his cheek to the corner of his mouth. He tilted his head ever so slightly, and their mouths met. Maybe it was better because he hadn't planned it, hadn't even thought about it, instead had been working through everything he needed to in order to get his attitude right. He hadn't seen this coming. But he'd wanted it. Had wanted it for a while. And, it seemed like as his attitude shifted and he got himself going in the right direction, other things fell into place too.

Later he might wonder if that was the Lord's way of saying that when he got himself right, let go of the things he knew he needed to, and allowed God to have His way, God could move. But currently, he was too swept away by Sally's lips moving against his, her hand on his face, her soft sigh and the way her hair flowed over his fingers as he put his hand on her neck and moved it down her back, trying to get her closer.

She pulled away just a little.

"This might be dangerous."

"Me kissing you in my house in the middle of the night? Yeah. Very dangerous."

She pressed her lips against his cheek, and he swallowed the disappointment that she didn't move them so that they met his again.

She was right. It was probably better that way.

"I love you," she said as her hands cupped both of his cheeks and she searched his eyes in the dim light. "And I don't care."

"You don't care about what?" he asked, feeling like there was a little bit of brain fog moving around in his head, and he couldn't quite follow her logic.

"What the doctor says. What your leg is like. What repercussions the concussion has. I just want you."

That was exactly what he wanted too. Just her. He wanted to be more for her though. To be someone she deserved, and not someone she had to settle for, but that was what she was saying. She wasn't settling. She was getting what she wanted.

"I'm yours," he said, lifting one shoulder. "But I don't feel like you're getting much."

"I'm getting everything I wanted," she said, smiling into his eyes, and there was no doubt that she was happy.

"I think I'm getting the better end of this deal, but I'm not going to argue with you.

If you're willing to take me, just as I am, I'm fine with it."

She smiled, and then she kissed him again, and he was definitely feeling the brain fog when she finally slipped away, and hurried back up the stairs.

He figured in the morning he'd probably feel like it was a dream, but for now, he fell asleep smiling.

Chapter 17

"Here, let me," Peter said, holding out his hand as they reached the bottom of the porch steps.

Sally smiled, putting her hand into his, and looking into his eyes. She was tempted to allow her gaze to go down, to see the leg that no longer had a cast, but she always had trouble getting lost in Peter's eyes.

They grinned together as he helped her up the steps for the first time in six weeks.

"I can definitely get used to this," he said, as they reached the top. He was slightly out of breath, which Sally figured was normal. He hadn't used his leg for a long time, and the muscles had atrophied. He would have to build them back up again, but the fact that the cast was off was the exciting thing of the day. All the work that lay ahead of them was mild in comparison to that.

"Have you told Miles?" Sally asked, knowing that Peter was beyond excited to be able to jump back into the farm work.

"No. I didn't want to jinx anything on the way to the doctors this morning. I knew they were going to take one last x-ray, and I could just see me telling Miles that I was getting my cast off, and then it end up being that the doc was going to say I had to wear a whole body cast for the next eight weeks or something."

"I don't think we've been together long enough for me to actually attack you with a skillet and put you in a body cast. But I'll keep it in mind," Sally said, grinning at him. Both of them knew that she would never go after him with a skillet or anything else for that matter.

"All right. Note to self, remove all iron cookware from the kitchen."

They laughed together as they walked in the house.

Sally, while over the moon happy for Peter, was a little sad. She felt like it was justifiable for her to stay at his house while he had his leg casted and needed help. But now that he was whole, she was moving out. Her things were all packed, it was just a matter of her bringing them down the stairs and walking out.

She was going to miss spending so much time with him. Of course, he would be back out working on the farm, and wouldn't be hanging around the house anyway, but still.

"I'm going to miss you," Peter said, as they walked to the kitchen, where Sally put her purse on the counter and washed her hands.

"I didn't want to say anything. I'm happy for you, truly I am, but I'm going to miss being able to spend so much time with you."

"You know if we got married, we'd be able to spend as much time as we wanted together."

"That's true," she said, her voice coming out as casually as she could make it, but her heart flipping and skipping inside of her chest. What was he saying? Was it just a casual statement? Or was he saying something more?

His hand came down on her shoulder, and he turned her as she dried her hands on the dish towel.

"I'm sorry, that was pretty backhanded and very awkward, wasn't it?"

"I don't know. Was it?"

"I wanted to ask you to marry me. I... I don't have a ring, I wasn't really even planning on it, but the idea of having you leave is just...hard."

"Well, sometimes I believe we have to go through hard things, and sometimes we can get married instead," Sally said with a laugh.

"Wow. This proposal really went off the rails."

"We could try again. You want me to get down on my knee?" Sally asked, throwing the tea towel on the counter and putting a hand on either side of Peter's waist. There was a comfort she drew from the contact, that she didn't recall feeling with anyone else. Ever.

"How about I do it? The only problem is, I don't have a little box to open up at the right time."

"Maybe you've watched too many sappy romantic movies with me over the last six weeks."

"Maybe I haven't seen enough, since I was obviously not prepared for the direction this conversation has taken."

"Well, I'm not sure exactly what direction it is, so let me take the conversation by the horns and just flat out say, Peter, I love you. Will you marry me?"

He tilted his head, as though he were thinking about it, or maybe as though he expected her to actually be on one knee.

She dropped, keeping her hands at his waist, as she gazed up into his eyes, and said, "Please?"

"I think if you have to beg someone to marry you, marriage might not be a good idea."

He dropped down so that they were face to face again. "But you don't have to beg me to do anything. In fact, it's most likely going to be me begging you. Can we get married? And soon? Like... Today?"

She laughed. Loving that they could have serious conversations, but they could goof off with each other too. She wasn't quite sure how she'd gotten so blessed, but she knew she was. She also knew she was making a good choice. Peter had shown her over the last six weeks that not only was he willing to take whatever the Lord gave him, and make the best of it, but that he would try that as hard as he could to choose happiness as well.

"Tomorrow's fine. Today is better," she said.

"And I think that a question like that is supposed to be sealed with a kiss."

"I agree," she said.

He leaned forward, and she pressed against him, their lips meeting, and she forgot that they were on their knees in the kitchen with both of them starving. Kissing Peter made her forget unimportant things like that.

"Hey! Are you guys okay?"

The voice startled her, and she pulled back, although not too far. Being close to Peter was the best place to be at any time, in her opinion anyway.

"Miles. What's up?" Peter asked, glancing over his shoulder at his friend, and then back to Sally.

He stood, a little awkwardly since he wasn't used to using his leg, and then he helped Sally to her feet as well.

"Norma Jean!" Sally said, pleased to see her friend standing just behind Miles.

Over the last six weeks, she'd gone from seeming to want to spend all of her time with Peter, to appearing content helping Miles. Sally really hadn't seen much of her. There had been so much work to do, plus watching Holly, who stood beside them now.

"So you did get your cast off," Miles said, grinning.

"I sure did," Peter turned, putting his arm around Sally's waist and pulling her toward him. "And I also asked Sally to marry me. She's agreed."

"It was actually me asking him. And I talked him into it," Sally said.

"Interesting. Funny, since Norma Jean and I just got hitched at the courthouse this morning."

"You what?" Sally said, not seeing that coming at all.

"I need a mom for my daughter, and Norma Jean needed a few things that I could give her, so we have an arrangement."

Norma Jean didn't exactly look like she was glowing, and in fact she came forward slowly.

"And I have a confession to make."

Sally felt dread, hot and heavy, settle into her stomach.

Then her eyes slipped to Miles, who looked surprised. They hadn't stopped in for whatever it was that Norma Jean was about to say.

"Confession is good for the soul, so they say," Sally said, hoping to put Norma Jean at ease.

"I'm afraid you guys are going to hate me."

"We aren't going to hate you," Peter said, and Sally squeezed him closer. She knew he meant that. And it made her heart sing.

"I left the gate open on purpose. I was hoping that Peter would come up and put cows in and give me some attention. It was... Stupid. I understand that I might owe you the cost of your medical bills, and whatever else you want me to pay. I'll work for the rest of my life to pay it off if that's what I have to do."

"What?" Miles's voice sounded threatening as he walked from where he stood at the door toward the kitchen.

Norma Jean turned toward him. "I should have told you before we did what we did this morning. I'm sorry. I understand if you... Want to get an annulment or something."

"We can't just pretend we didn't say vows," Miles said, and he didn't sound happy about it. "Yeah. That definitely was something that you should have told me. I shouldn't be finding out now in front of everyone else."

"I'm sorry," Norma Jean said.

Sally felt terrible for her. Norma Jean was strong and tough, and Sally couldn't remember ever seeing her cry, but her voice wobbled now.

Miles didn't say anything more, but a muscle in his cheek moved back and forth, and a vein popped out in his temple as he stared at his new wife.

Finally, he looked over at Sally and Peter. "Congratulations. If you need me, you know where I'll be...with my...wife." He spit the word out, none too gently, and then, he lifted his brows at Norma Jean as though asking if she was ready to go.

She lifted her chin, and Sally's heart went out to her at the look she gave her husband. Sally managed to keep from putting her hand over her mouth, but from that look, Sally was sure that Norma Jean was in love with Miles. Unfortunately, it sounded like her marriage wasn't a love match, and Norma Jean had definitely started things out in the worst possible way.

Sally hoped their marriage could survive, but... It was hard enough to stay married in a regular relationship, let alone when the marriage started out with one person keeping a secret from another, and then offending them by telling other people something that their spouse should have already known.

But, Sally couldn't fix that at all, although she watched with sadness as Norma Jean turned, took Holly's hand, and walked out the door in front of Miles, whose shoulders were stiff and filled with tension.

"I think Miles has it bad for her," Peter said as the door closed behind them.

"You're kidding. And here I was thinking that Norma Jean was infatuated with Miles, and I felt bad for her."

Peter laughed. "Maybe you're right. I've just...never seen Miles like that. I'd say he is head over heels. But he swore he wasn't getting married again, and maybe he did that so she wouldn't get away."

The idea of some man not wanting Norma Jean to get away was kind of a new idea and a little odd, but Sally hoped it was true.

"I think they'll be able to work things out," Peter said.

"I'd love to be a fly on the wall following them around for a little while, because... I think they could have a really interesting love story."

"The way you and I do."

"I think ours was pretty easy. All I had to do was get you to break your leg, have a concussion, and be stuck on the couch for six weeks, and presto, you have no choice but to fall in love with me."

"It was that easy?"

"Yeah. You should really think about playing hard to get some time."

"I suppose me reminding you that you said we could get married tomorrow is not me playing hard to get?"

"No. But, maybe you can start after that."

"Or maybe I could just kiss you instead. That sounds like a lot more fun to me."

"Me too," Sally said, and she forgot about lunch as she moved to put her arms around Peter and lifted her head as he lowered his lips toward hers.

It seemed like maybe both of them had decided to choose happiness, which was a lot easier when a person got to be with the one they loved.

Thanks so much for reading There I Find Happiness and spending a little time in Strawberry Sands. If you'd like to see some of your favorite characters return and meet some wonderful new folk just up the beach in Raspberry Ridge, I'd love for you to order the first book in my Raspberry Ridge series, On the Sandy Beach.

newsletter – I laughed so hard I sprayed it out all over the table!"

Claim your free book from Jessie!